Letter from the Publisher,

I am proud to announce the newest Tyler-Lanier publication, *Greater Outdoors Magazine*. I am especially thrilled that *Greater Outdoors* will be featuring the work of noted wildlife photographer Tonya Griffin.

Publisher Web Tyler is thrilled to welcome Ms. Griffin (strange how I feel like we've met before, and why do I keep associating her with the back of a limousine?) to the Tyler-Lanier family (but first I have to get her to sign an exclusive contract—not an easy task, since I think she hates me).

The winner of several prestigious awards, Ms. Griffin is one of the most-sought-after photographers in her field (and a hottie to boot). She is eager to share her work with the *Greater Outdoors* readers (but she just might kill me before the first roll of film is developed!).

Sincerely,

Web Tyler

Publisher

Dear Reader,

We're so glad you've chosen Silhouette Desire because we have a *lot* of wonderful—and sexy!—stories for you. The month starts to heat up with *The Boss Man's Fortune* by Kathryn Jensen. This fabulous boss/secretary novel is part of our ongoing continuity, DYNASTIES: THE DANFORTHS, and also reintroduces characters from another well-known family: The Fortunes. Things continue to simmer with Peggy Moreland's *The Last Good Man in Texas,* a fabulous continuation of her series THE TANNERS OF TEXAS.

More steamy stuff is heading your way with *Shut Up And Kiss Me* by Sara Orwig, as she starts off a new series, STALLION PASS: TEXAS KNIGHTS. (Watch for the series to continue next month in Silhouette Intimate Moments.) The always-compelling Laura Wright is back with a hot-blooded Native American hero in *Redwolf's Woman. Storm of Seduction* by Cindy Gerard will surely fire up your hormones with an alpha male hero out of your wildest fantasies. And Margaret Allison makes her Silhouette Desire debut with *At Any Price,* a book about sweet revenge that is almost too hot to handle!

And, as summer approaches, we'll have more scorching love stories for you—guaranteed to satisfy your every Silhouette Desire!

Happy reading,

Melissa Jeglinski

Melissa Jeglinski
Senior Editor, Silhouette Desire

Please address questions and book requests to:
Silhouette Reader Service
U.S.: 3010 Walden Ave., P.O. Box 1325, Buffalo, NY 14269
Canadian: P.O. Box 609, Fort Erie, Ont. L2A 5X3

Storm of Seduction

CINDY GERARD

Silhouette® Desire

Published by Silhouette Books

America's Publisher of Contemporary Romance

SILHOUETTE BOOKS

ISBN 0-373-76583-5

STORM OF SEDUCTION

Copyright © 2004 by Cindy Gerard

This edition published by arrangement with Harlequin Books S.A.

® and TM are trademarks of Harlequin Books S.A., used under license. Trademarks indicated with ® are registered in the United States Patent and Trademark Office, the Canadian Trade Marks Office and in other countries.

Visit Silhouette Books at www.eHarlequin.com

Printed in U.S.A.

Books by Cindy Gerard

CINDY GERARD

Since her first release in 1991 hit the national #1 slot on the Waldenbooks bestseller list, Cindy Gerard has repeatedly made appearances on several bestseller lists, including *USA TODAY*. With numerous industry awards to her credit—among them the Romance Writers of America's RITA® Award and the National Reader's Choice Award—this former Golden Heart Finalist and repeat *Romantic Times* nominee is the real deal.

Cindy and her husband, Tom, live in the Midwest on a minifarm with quarter horses, cats and two very spoiled dogs. When she's not writing, she enjoys reading, traveling and spending time at their cabin in northern Minnesota unwinding with family and friends. Cindy loves to hear from her readers and invites you to visit her Web site at www.cindygerard.com.

This book is dedicated to friends.
Old ones. New ones. Tried and true ones. I am blessed.

One

She was in love. Desperately in love. A woman in love sometimes did reprehensible things, committed unforgivable acts—all in the name of love.

Tucking herself deeper in the forest shadows, Tonya Griffin prayed the elusive Damien didn't see her—thanked the powers that be she'd finally spotted him again. The first time she'd seen him a little over a week ago, she'd fallen for him like a collapsing castle of cards. She'd been hoping for another glimpse of him ever since.

In the name of love, she forgave herself for breaching his privacy and exploiting his trust. She lifted her camera, made adjustments for the September sunlight, and focused.

"Caught you, you coldhearted devil," she whispered and, carefully sidestepping a white pine, aimed her lens for an unobstructed view.

He wasn't aware that she was following him, or that she was filming him—yet. She knew, however, that he'd sense her presence soon enough, so she moved fast before she lost the late-afternoon light or before the storm forecast for later this afternoon blew in. She also needed to work fast before he discovered what she was doing and disappeared again. Oh, he wouldn't like it. Wouldn't like it at all that she'd captured him in any way—even if it was just on film.

"Forgive me, Damien," she apologized without ever losing focus, and zoomed a little closer.

The definition the close-up shot provided sent a shiver down her spine even though it was a warm Indian summer day. He was truly magnificent. His keen eyes, as dark as the luxurious pelt of obsidian-black hair matting his chest, searched the forest of pine and ash as he stood tall—well over six feet.

"Mr. Tall, Dark and Dangerous," she murmured with a loving smile. "Master of your universe, aren't you, big guy?"

His head whipped around her way. With a low growl, he spotted her.

"Uh-oh." She lowered the camera, held her breath—and understood that she had suddenly become the hunted.

Her heart tripped over itself, then settled into a rabbit-run beat that thundered through her chest and pounded in her ears like the waves pummeling the rocky lakeshore a hundred or so yards in the distance.

Dangerous.

The word echoed a warning shot through her mind even as she raised the camera again, snapping off a rapid succession of frames.

His angry snarl shook the forest floor of decaying leaves and pine needles and shocked the air like an ozone burst before a sunset storm. Utterly still—in truth, frozen to the spot—Tonya stood in the fractured silence as he stomped two charging strides toward her. A reminder of who ruled here. A caution that she had gone too far.

It occurred to her then that she could die here. She wouldn't be missed for weeks. And suddenly, she felt very alone and very afraid. Buried beneath the panic, she felt a twinge of regret for all the things she'd wanted to do with her life. For all the things she'd missed. And then she quit thinking at all as he took another menacing step forward.

Air stalled in her lungs; her heart slammed against her sternum. She braced for the blow that would surely come when, unbelievably, he made an abrupt stop and spun away.

Her breath came back on a whoosh as he stormed off into a copse of pine and birch so dense it swallowed him up before he'd taken more than four powerful strides.

The telltale tingling in her fingertips alerted her to her death grip on her camera.

The pressure on her bladder rudely informed her how scared she'd been.

A tight laugh rippled out. Nerves. Relief.

"He loves me," she murmured on a quivering smile and, turning, headed at a fast walk, back toward the cabin.

"Got to be love," she reasoned, cruising on a latent burst of adrenaline and upped her speed to a jog when she finally spotted a curl of smoke rising from the little log cabin nestled in the clearing about a quarter mile ahead. "Gotta be—or I'd be dead right now instead of wondering if I can make it to the john before I pee my pants."

In spite of the close call, in spite of her pressing need, she laughed at the utter joy of catching Damien in the wild—all six-hundred-plus pounds of him. He was, without a doubt, the biggest, baddest most beautiful black bear in Koochiching County, Minnesota, and for a moment there—just for a moment—he'd been hers.

"Unbelievable," Web Tyler muttered under his breath as the laughing woman bolted out of the forest and blew right by him. Tonya Griffin didn't so much as bat one of those baby blues his way.

At least he figured it was the reclusive Ms. Griffin. He'd never met her. He'd seen pictures of the award-winning wildlife photographer though—usually black and whites and invariably distant grainy shots of her working in some remote corner of the globe. He knew her work though. Anyone who'd ever picked up a *National Geographic* or a dozen other wildlife magazines did. Just as everyone knew her talent was first-rate.

That's why he was here. Tonya Griffin was the best. Since Web needed the best, he'd grudgingly left civilization and a soft bed on a crack-of-dawn flight out of JFK to lure her out of the woods and into an exclusive contract with Tyler-Lanier Publishing. Things had been slipping down a steady decline ever since.

To start with, the company jet had been chartered so he'd had to fly commercial to Minnesota. Pearl, his executive secretary, had neglected to tell him about that little tidbit of info. After an interminable three-hour layover at the Minneapolis Airport, he'd squeezed into a puddle jumper for the two hour flight north to International Falls, Minnesota, a town of approximately ten thousand that sat right on the Canadian border. When no luxury cars had been available at the one and only rental-car agency, he'd had to settle for a well-worn compact.

And then things really started getting good. He'd been told it was a two-hour drive to the bear sanctuary where Tonya Griffin was hiding out in the woods. Two hours providing he didn't get lost. He had. Several times. Four hours and thirty-seven minutes later, he'd finally made it to where he'd wanted to be— relatively speaking—but not before he'd damn near buried the rental in a pothole roughly the size of Alaska. The car had been making a strange noise ever since, sort of a *tick, whoosh, tick, whoosh* that he'd chosen to ignore because he really didn't have any other options anyway. He was no ace mechanic. Just as he was no pathfinder—or outdoorsman.

Hands on his hips, he looked grimly around him, then shook his head on a weary sigh. He was so far off his regular flight path the distance couldn't even be calculated in miles. An urban dweller to the bone, he couldn't wait to end this little close encounter with the land of moose and mosquitoes. And as he stood there, surrounded by rock, trees and sky, and the biggest silence he'd ever heard, the obvious question now was, *what in the hell had he been thinking?*

Survival. That's what he'd been thinking. His professional survival. At least his professional reputation. To insure it, he needed Tonya Griffin—whether she wanted to be a part of his game plan or not.

He let out a breath through puffed cheeks and tracked her with his gaze, intrigued by the woman in spite of himself. How could she *not* have seen him standing at the edge of the clearing? It was baffling as hell, and yet, he gave up a grudging smile at the single-minded concentration that led her right past him as if he were invisible. Yeah. As if he didn't stand six feet one and fill up a substantial portion of her immediate viewing area.

Rather than announce himself at this point, he kept his silence as his head swiveled, tracking her as she streaked toward an ancient log cabin nestled in the clearing.

"What ever happened to hello?" he mumbled after she disappeared inside.

For a long moment, he stared at the closed door. "Okay, hotshot. What now?"

Now, apparently, he waited. He was on a mission

of diplomacy. A mission on which his professional reputation depended.

"You're here to make nice," he reminded himself under his breath and reset his mind to grudgingly tolerate the woman's rumored hermitlike eccentricities.

Well, he was tolerating. Hell, he was here, wasn't he? Point for him. He was tolerating and inexplicably waiting to charm a woman who, he had no doubt, was going to prove to be a colossal pain in the ass.

He leaned down and picked up the camouflage ball cap that had flown off her head on her way by. Yeah, he thought as he swatted a mosquito from his neck, he was definitely tolerating.

The sound of a slamming door brought his head up and his gaze toward the ancient log cabin. The reason for his foray into *Camp Nowhere He Wanted To Be* stood on the top step of the stoop, staring him straight in the eye, a scowl as dark as thunder turning her baby blues to smoky cobalt.

"You're on private property."

Well, he thought, apparently he was also in hostile territory. He managed to dredge up a smile. It wasn't really so hard to smile at her. It was never hard to smile at a woman and while this one wasn't beautiful, she was passably pretty in an outdoorsy, all-American girl sort of way. "And you're a hard woman to find."

She crossed her arms over her breasts and eyed him with suspicion. "Apparently not hard enough."

He took a step forward, extended his hand. "I'm Web Tyler."

She didn't budge a step to meet him halfway. Neither did she offer her hand. She did, however, snag the cap from his hand. "I know who you are."

"Great," he said, not surprised that she knew of him. "Then I'll spare you the résumé. And here's a nice twist—I know who you are, too."

She watched him for a silent moment before expelling what was clearly an annoyed breath. "What do you want, Tyler?"

To be anywhere but here, cupcake. "For starters? A cup of coffee would be great."

She leaned a hip against the porch rail and pointed her chin toward what could loosely be called a road. "Driftwood Café," she offered, unsmiling, "About twenty miles back the way you came, left side of the road. You can't miss it. The pie's good, too."

He was relatively sure she was right. He probably couldn't miss it considering he'd ended up at the four-corners crossroad where the Driftwood Café stood three times in his search for the correct turnoff. He couldn't help it. He laughed at his inability to follow directions, this ridiculous situation and her sour look. "Not exactly a paragon of hospitality, are you?"

"I'm working, Mr. Tyler. Social hour doesn't start for another five hours or so."

"Fine." He forced another amiable smile when she walked down the cabin steps and breezed by him for the second time today. "I'll wait until you're finished so we can talk."

She stalled, looked over her shoulder, then shrugged. "Suit yourself."

Mesmerized in spite of himself, he just stood there

as she went about her business around what could be loosely called a compound.

Late-afternoon sunshine set gold highlights flashing in the pale blond mane she'd wrestled into a single thick, untidy braid that hung midway down her back. While the bulk of it hit just between her shoulder blades, an abundance of lacy strands drifted softly around her face and tickled her nape. Bits and pieces of leaves and twigs had attached themselves to the flyaway silk like cobwebs. There were probably a few of those in there, too, he figured with a grunt of disapproval and walked over to the porch steps.

He sat down on the bottom tread, clasped his hands and propped his elbows on his knees, determined to wait her out. She'd have to deal with him sometime.

While he let his gaze drift around the clearing, it inevitably tracked straight back to her. Finally, he just gave it up and watched her, chalking up his interest in her physical persona to boredom, because, sure as the world, there wasn't much of anything else about the woman that would compel a man to take a second look.

Boredom. That pretty well summed things up. He hadn't been in this backwater spot in Nowhere, Minnesota more than a couple of hours, and he was already bored out of his mind. Bored by the trees, bored by the promise of solitude, bored by the infernal quiet of the woods. He already missed New York and the beat of the city, the lights and the speed. He couldn't afford to be away from the magazine for this long. But neither, according to Pearl, could he afford *not*

to make the trip in person to entice the inimitable
Tonya Griffin into the fold.

And yet, as he listened to her bang around in a
small shed then come out with armloads of pans filled
with what appeared to be dog food, he found himself
admiring the view. It was ridiculous. It baffled the
hell out of him that his libido would even wrap itself
around the image. She was *so* not his type. In fact,
he wasn't sure whose type she might be.

What kind of man, he wondered, would take a tumble for the pint-size photographer who preferred four-
legged carnivores to men, and whose wardrobe
clearly consisted of varying shades of khaki. She
probably threw in the occasional camouflage sweatshirt as a sort of survivalist's fashion statement just
to mix it up a bit. Hell, her attention to drab would
make the marines proud—especially when she topped
it all off with those mud-ugly, lace-up hiking boots.

He stretched his legs out in front of him, crossed
his ankles and propped his elbows on the step behind
him, prepared to settle in for the duration. She wasn't
completely successful in hiding the evidence that she
was, for a fact, very female. Through narrowed eyes,
he caught fleeting glimpses of a slight but sweet little
jiggle beneath the pockets of her shirt while she
breezed around. Intelligent man that he was, he took
it as a sure indicator that she had breasts. Possibly
nice ones, but it was apparent she had no intention of
showing them off to her advantage—or for any man's
appreciation.

He tilted his head, took a long look and decided

her legs weren't bad, either, if you ignored the welts from bug bites, the various scratches and bruises and the dirt smearing her knees. And then there was her butt. He had to admit, she had a premium butt. Even her baggy shorts couldn't hide that fact.

Hide seemed to be the operative word here. He may not know her, but he knew *of* her. Everything he'd been told about Tonya Griffin with the sweet breasts, decidedly fine butt and glossy tangle of angel hair, indicated she wanted to hide anything about herself that was remotely female. Just as her primary mission was hiding herself away from civilization like Jungle Jane or Amazon Lily and of late, Minnesota Moppet.

It went without saying that she was not the type of female he understood. Again, not that she wasn't marginally attractive. She had pretty blue eyes—eyes that probably sparkled when she laughed. He'd seen nothing but cobalt blue, like the color of the sky before a storm. Her lips were full and fairly lush, her nose was kind of cute, her forehead high, like her cheekbones. With a little makeup it would be hard to imagine what she could accomplish.

Those were the kind of women he understood. Women who knew how to artfully apply makeup, drape themselves in designer clothes and perfectly style their hair. He understood beautifully manicured nails, come-hither looks and stiletto heels. He appreciated sophistication, ambition and the game playing that went along with the urban dating scene.

He did *not* understand a woman who smelled like bug spray and whose only claim to sophistication was the pricey camera she'd been carrying when she'd blown by him out of the forest as if her tail was on fire. He did not understand a woman who, instead of coming on to him, would probably be perfectly content in the role of the most singularly annoying and major thorn in his side. Which she'd already become without even trying.

A half an hour passed before he lost patience and decided to see if he couldn't get her to hold still long enough to engage her in some semblance of conversation. He wanted to get her signed and get out of here. He'd just stood and wiped the dust off the seat of his pants when the hair on the back of his neck suddenly stood at attention.

He was being watched. By what, or whom, he didn't know, but since his information indicated that no one but Tonya was currently residing out here, it narrowed down the options pretty fast.

Slowly, he turned his head. And froze.

Not six feet away, a black bear that looked big enough and hungry enough to take him out in one bloody chomp stood on his hind legs and uttered a low, rumbling growl.

Every muscle in his body tensed with the instinct to run like hell. He was about to break into the fastest sprint of his life when he sensed another presence.

"Don't move," he heard his reluctant hostess say in a very soft, very calm, but deadly serious voice from a few feet away. He hadn't heard her approach any more than he'd heard the bear.

Right now he didn't hear much of anything but the

warning growl and the sound of blood rushing through his ears. And while his first instinct had been to move and move fast, the truth of the matter was, he was pretty much frozen to the spot. The bear with the humungous teeth and razor-sharp claws was sizing him up with diamond black eyes and a series of grunting sniffs.

"Do you have any food on you?"

Eyes never leaving the big black dude, who was clearly considering him for the entrée on tonight's menu, Web tried to think. "No. Wait. Thin mints," he said, finally remembering popping for the chocolate candy at an airport vending machine.

"Very slowly take them out of your pocket. No quick moves. Now, toss them a few yards away. Good. Slowly hold up your hands, palms out, to show him they're empty."

Web did exactly as she instructed, then watched in suspended silence as the big boar gave him a last, inquisitive sniff before ambling off to scoop up the candy. With amazing dexterity, the bear ripped open the package, scarfed down the chocolate then lumbered down a path to one of the pans of dog food she'd set around the clearing.

When he could find enough lung power to breathe, he sucked in air, latched on to his frazzled dignity and somehow managed a smile. "Wilderness survival lesson number one," he said, turning his attention back to her scowling face, "never stand between a bear and his snack. Unless you want to *be* the snack."

While the joke did the job of calming him, it was a wasted attempt to charm her.

"Lesson number two. You only get one shot at passing lesson number one." She walked around him and scooted back up the cabin steps, hooking her thumb in the general direction of the road as she went by. "Oscar is the first of many bears who will be wandering in for their sunset snack within the next hour or so. They aren't all as friendly. If I were you I'd quit while I was ahead. The highway and civilization are that way."

He stared at the door she closed behind her. Ran a hand through his hair—embarrassed to find it was still a little shaky.

"Are we having fun yet, Tyler?" he grumbled, and stomped up the steps after her, making a quick check to ensure the bear was still lumbering away in the opposite direction.

No, we were *not* having fun. So far, he'd been bullied into leaving New York, driven around in circles in a garbage can on wheels, gotten lost for hours in territory as foreign as outer space, only to be greeted by a muddy-kneed militant in combat boots who had grudgingly saved his greenhorn hide from being fodder for a bear's bone pile.

Definitely not fun. In fact, while he'd been mildly irritated before, he was damn close to being pissed off now. It wasn't just that he was out of his element. It wasn't even that she was too rude to even listen to his proposal. It was, he realized, the fact that command and control—components he usually owned in any negotiation—were hers, not his.

And that ticked him off. Royally.

This was her turf. Boardrooms, bedrooms, dinner at the Plaza, bull and bear markets—those were his. He didn't deal with rutted dirt roads, log cabins, acres and acres of trees and real bears, for God's sake. He didn't deal with out-of-hand denials.

And that, as far as he was concerned, was Ms. Griffin's fatal error. He didn't like to be told no. He especially didn't like to be told no without ever having had a chance to present his argument.

He may not be happy about being here. He may not be used to rejection, but he was a long way from packing up his toys and hightailing it toward home. She said she knew who he was. If she really knew him, she'd know one very important thing about him—he didn't always play fair but he always played to win, and this game was far from over.

Somehow, he was going to find a way to drag Tonya Griffin back to New York. In fact, the idea of knocking some of the pine needles off the prickly photographer made him smile—the same polished smile that had swung as many boardroom votes as it had women his way.

He mentally rubbed his hands together with determination as he walked up the steps. He'd do the job and then get out of Dodge. *Okay, Ms. Get-your-city-boy-self-out-of-my-face Griffin. Let the games begin.*

Two

Just as Web lifted his hand to knock on the cabin door, his cell phone vibrated in his pocket. He fished it out, saw the name on the screen and expelled a weary breath.

"Yes, Pearl," he said, digging for patience.

He sank down on the top tread of the cabin steps as Pearl Reasoner's steel-and-orchid voice asked him about his flight and whether or not he'd found Tonya Griffin. Pearl, in addition to being his executive secretary, also happened to be his godmother. Of late, she was also the cause for the recurrent throbbing in his right temple.

He'd wanted to send his executive officer, Price, or his vice president, Hawkins, to handle this. But Pearl had insisted he was the one who needed to fly to

Minnesota to play Dr. Livingston-I-Presume and convince Tonya Griffin to sign an exclusive contract to get his new baby, *Greater Outdoors* magazine, off the ground.

The scene with Pearl in his office yesterday—the one that had landed him here—played out in his mind's eye as Pearl droned on about R and R, fresh air and glacial lakes. Northern Minnesota was a helluva long way from Tyler-Lanier Publishing Group's fifty-eighth floor suite of offices on Sixth Avenue, and still his argument that he was a publisher, not a lumberjack had fallen on deaf ears.

"As publisher the buck stops with you. You want to land the C. C. Bozeman account, then you need Tonya Griffin. If her photography isn't featured in the premier issue of Greater Outdoors, *then Bozeman doesn't buy advertising space in the magazine. If we lose C. C. Bozeman Outdoor gear, we're sunk before we even hit the water."*

His insistence that he didn't have time for a wilderness adventure had prompted a deep sigh and an indictment of his current state of health.

"Webster, you are burned out, tapped out and played out with all the transitions that have been happening in-house since the merger. If nothing else, the break will do you good."

Pearl continued to drone on enthusiastically about how he really should enjoy the fishing as long as he was there.

He stared at the copse of trees in front of him and tried to ignore both Pearl—who he loved in spite of her interference—and the image he faced in the mirror each morning lately. He wasn't sure he liked what he saw these days any more than she did. His brown eyes were flat with—with what? Fatigue? Disinterest? Regrets? So he worked hard. So he was disenchanted with the rat race. So at the age of thirty-five, he'd exceeded all of his monetary goals and yet he felt as if there had to be more. Something. Anything.

He didn't figure he was going to find that *something* in Northern Minnesota. He sure as hell wasn't going to find it scrabbling after the photographer famous not only for her work, but for her aversion to anything that remotely resembled civilization.

"I'm assuming you heard about Jimmy Lawler in accounting."

Pearl's monologue broke through his thoughts. He could see her standing there, lording over his desk now that he was gone. She was seventy if she was a day, but the most he'd ever heard her admit to was fifty-eight. With her keen green eyes, artfully styled auburn hair and impeccable makeup, she could pull it off, no problem.

"Forty years old," she stated with meaning, then paused to make sure she had his attention. "Keeled over dead last week. Heart attack. Know what his tombstone's *not* going to say? *I wish I'd spent more time at the office.*"

Web thought about Tonya Griffin, holed up in the cabin behind him.

"Webster—"

"I'm *here,* okay?" he said, because sometimes it

was just easier to give in. And because, ultimately, Pearl had been right. He did need Tonya Griffin if he was going to hit the ground running with *Greater Outdoors.* "Can't you be satisfied with that?"

"Only if you promise to stay where you are for at least two weeks. I mean, as long as you're there, take advantage of the downtime. Two weeks will be soon enough to get her back here, set up the shoots and keep on our timetable for the first issue to hit the stands in six months—but just enough time. Sweetie, I tucked some brochures in your carry-on. Did you find them?"

Yeah, he'd found them. Glossy pictures of a north woods lodge near the Minnesota-Canadian border. More pictures of beaming fishermen with sunburns and baseball caps hefting plump stringers of fish.

"For the last time, Pearl, I do not fish. I do not intend to fish. For God's sake, they've got mosquitoes up here that could give a vampire a run for his money. And there are bears, Pearl. Real bears with teeth and claws and huge appetites for citified meat and chocolate. One of them damn near ate me not less than five minutes ago. So I'll come back as soon as I can get this woman's tree-hugging butt out of the boonies and onto the assignments we have lined up for her."

"Two weeks and not a day sooner," Pearl insisted in that tone that held affection, iron will and a *don't cross me on this, boyo* determination. "You're all set for clothes, after all."

He wiped a hand over his face. Oh, yeah, he was set. Pearl had taken the liberty of buying out C. C.

Bozeman's downtown store and having the goods messengered over to his co-op. Everything had been waiting for him when he'd gotten home last night. He hadn't wasted a glare at the confidence that had prompted her to make arrangements prior to his nod of consent as he'd stuffed everything in his brand new C. C. Bozeman wilderness travel duffel bag.

"A week," he said, because, after all, he *was* the boss—at least he was when Pearl allowed him the luxury of thinking so, "but I swear, if you say one more word—"

"Deal. Now don't pout, Webster. You're there now, aren't you? We've accomplished enough for one day."

"*We* haven't accomplished anything. You, on the other hand—"

"Have moved the immovable object. I know, dear. And believe me, it was exhausting."

Yeah. It was exhausting all right. Just as it was exhausting thinking about butting heads with another object that clearly did not have any inclination to being moved by him.

He, however, moved damn fast up the steps when he spotted another bear lumber into the clearing and amble over to a pan of food.

How the heck did she live like this? He'd take his chances with a mugger any day over these bears. At least he generally knew their motives: they wanted money. With these bears, who knew what would provoke them. Hell. They'd take a guy out for a thin mint.

Pearl could forget about his week-long vacation. He'd be on a flight out of here by midnight with a signed contract in his hands—while he still *had* both hands.

Tonya held a banged-up copper teakettle under the slow-running tap and tried to ignore the fact that her hand was shaking. Web Tyler. He was the last man she'd expected to see out here. He was the last man she'd expected to see anywhere. In fact, she'd made a second career of avoiding men like him.

Okay, she admitted as she lit a match to the burner on the ancient apartment-size gas cooking stove and set the kettle on to boil. She'd made a second career of avoiding *him,* not men like him.

Web Tyler was the grandson of Fulton Tyler of the infamous Tyler-Lanier Publishing Group based in New York. He was also her former employer and the source of one of the most embarrassing moments of her life.

She glanced over her shoulder toward the cabin's front door and felt her heart pound hard in her chest. She told herself to get a grip. Told herself to get over the blow to her ego that his lack of recognition had landed.

"Plain ol' forgettable me," she mumbled, and knocked around in the tiny cupboard for a coffee mug. In the process, she saw her reflection in the window above the sink and immediately felt like throwing up.

Twelve years. It had been twelve years since she'd

last seen Web Tyler. Given the fact that he published magazines and she sold her photographs to magazines, she'd always known she'd run into him again one day—no matter how hard she'd worked to avoid it. She'd even pictured the confrontation in her mind. Many times. The scene had always played out the same: She'd be impeccably groomed. She'd be the picture of successful, professional presence and style. And he would be stunned to see the woman she'd become.

Well, she figured he was stunned all right. She reached up and dragged a leaf out of her hair. A twig came with it. With a roll of her eyes, she tossed both in the trash then used the dish towel to scrub the dirt from her chin. She considered having a go at her legs then literally threw in the towel. Nothing short of a day at Elizabeth Arden was going to clean her up. And nothing less than a miracle was going to make this all go away.

With reluctance, she walked to the window, hooked a corner of the faded blue gingham curtain with her pinkie and sneaked a peek outside. He was on the stoop, talking on his cell phone, looking grim in profile—looking every bit the man she had tried to forget.

God, he was gorgeous. The only thing the years had added to his intriguing package was depth. Depth to his rich brown eyes, depth to the utterly masculine lines of his beautifully sculpted face. Depth to the dominant male presence he'd made a down payment on in his twenties and now owned in his mid-thirties.

And the fact that he'd shown up here out of the blue, catching her off guard, catching her looking like something the cat wouldn't bother to drag in, had rattled her good. Rattled her to the point where she was cowering inside the cabin like a ninny when she'd never run away from a confrontation in her life.

Behind her, the kettle whistled. She hurried back to the stove and turned off the fire. Then taking a bracing breath, she headed for the door. Odds are he wasn't going away until he had his say anyway, and the truth was, now that she was past her initial shock, she hated that she'd behaved like a coward.

Plus, curiosity was getting the best of her. What was Web Tyler—publishing mogul extraordinaire, urbanite to the bone, a man who had minions who hired minions to do his work—doing in the Northern Minnesota wilderness? And why had he gone to such great lengths to find her?

He was pocketing his cell phone with one hand and lifting the other to knock when she wrenched open the cabin door.

"Well," he said, looking startled and wary. "Hello, again."

"If you'll settle for tea," she said without preamble, "you're welcome to a cup. Herbal," she added, almost on a dare.

"Sounds great."

She gave him a *sure it does* look which only made him grin, which made her nervous. So nervous she turned and left him standing in the open doorway.

Trying not to be overly conscious of the sound of

him shutting the door behind him—or the fact that he was most likely watching every move she made—she snagged an extra mug from the cupboard, did a quick check to make sure it was clean, then filled both mugs with hot water.

"So," he said, as she set the mugs on a small chrome table with a gray Formica top that was marred with chips and scratches and the occasional burn mark. "This is home sweet home."

"For the time being." She grabbed a couple of spoons from the drawer that dragged on sticky skids. Bumping it shut with the help of her hip, she tracked his gaze as he slowly surveyed the small cabin, seeing it again as she'd first seen it almost a month ago.

Rustic was a fitting word to describe it. Spartan was another. Like many north-woods cabins, it was a one-room affair with the exception of a tiny bathroom that had been added several years after the cabin had been built sometime in the late 1930s.

The walls were knotty pine darkened by age to a warm honey-brown. The floors were also pine—worn, scarred and dulled to a tawny buff. A huge braided rug—Lord only knew how old—in muted colors of rust and gray and soft blue, covered all but the outer edge of the approximately twenty-by-twenty interior.

The kitchen—such as it was—consisted of a short wall of pine cabinets someone had painted royal blue many years ago, a small cast-iron sink, a chipped gas stove that could only be lit with the help of a match, and a Norge refrigerator, circa 1960, that needed to be defrosted every week or the frost on the small freezer grew stalactites.

In the middle of the room was the dining table at which Web Tyler sat. Tonya had picked some wild-flowers earlier in the week. They'd been pretty two days ago, vibrant yellows and burnt oranges and pristine whites. Today they were just sad reminders of how sidetracked she'd gotten with her work. So was the unmade double bed that butted up against the north wall and doubled as a sofa when there was a need. Since she generally worked from dawn to dusk and few souls ventured into this neck of Charlie Erickson's woods, there rarely was. On the opposite wall a small cast-iron woodstove, its embers banked and burning low in preparation for the cool night ahead, sat on a square of bricks dusted with ash.

Yeah. It was Spartan. But it had electricity and a working phone when the lines weren't down, so it was also palatial when compared to some of the mud-hut, dirt-floor accommodations she'd experienced in her travels around the world. Clearly, however, Web Tyler, a man used to Italian marble, imported rugs and art-gallery decor, considered it several steps down from urban decay.

She pulled out a chair—more faded gray and chrome—and, setting a spoon by his mug, opened the small tin canister containing her favorite tea.

"Chamomile and mint with a little rose hip," she told him with an arched eyebrow.

"Sounds serene," he finally said, and, for some

reason, his choice of words and the veiled tolerance with which he uttered them, had her fighting a smile.

"How did you find me?" she asked as he dipped his tea bag into the steaming water like a proper English gentlemen taking tea with his maiden aunt. "And we'll follow up with, *why* did you find me?"

"I didn't find you. My secretary did. Your agent gave you up. Which leads to the *why* part of your question. I have work for you, if you're interested."

"I'm not." She dipped her tea bag and reached for the sugar. "I already have work."

He leaned back, hooking an arm over the chair, his pose oozing confidence and control. "Whatever you're getting paid here, I'll double it."

This time she did smile.

He tilted his head, considered her. "And that's amusing because?"

She stirred her tea. "That's amusing because nothing doubled is still nothing. It's amusing because if money were a motivator I'd be doing fashion layouts or working in advertising."

"But you still have to eat, right? Why don't you hear me out before you close the door?"

After a careful sip of the hot tea, she met his eyes. "Look, Mr. Tyler—"

"Web."

"Web," she repeated after a moment's hesitation and wondered how many women besides her had gotten all tangled up inside just listening to the sound of his voice. Smooth as velvet, and like a full-bodied wine, it had only gotten richer with age.

And she should have gotten wiser.

"If you've got a shoot lined up you want me to consider, talk to my agent. He'll deal with you if he thinks it's something that will interest me. I don't know why you didn't just talk to him in the first place instead of coming all the way to Minnesota."

"I don't have a shoot for you," he said pointedly. "I have a job. And I tracked you down personally because I'd like to offer you an exclusive contract."

She slowly sipped more tea. Mingled with the subtle fragrance of chamomile and mint, his scent, a wholly masculine mix of man and spice and wealth invaded her senses. It had been a long time since she'd been aware of the scent of anything but fresh air and pine and mosquito spray. Longer still since she'd thought about the way expensive cologne reacted to the warmth of a man's skin, a long time since she'd missed being with a man and absorbing that intoxicating blend up close and personal.

Now was definitely not the time to miss it. Now was the time to… Whoa. Wait. What had he said?

"Excuse me?"

He leaned forward, tapped his thumb absently on the lip of the mug. "Exclusive contract. Tyler-Lanier. Yes. You heard me right."

She looked from his eyes—beautifully shifting shades of brown, cinnamon and mocha latte—to his hands, overly aware of the strength of both, and the enormity of his offer. Once she'd have pounced on it like a leopard on a field mouse. "Sorry, but you've wasted your time. I'm strictly freelance. I don't do exclusive for anyone.''

He frowned as if he really couldn't believe she'd said no. There wasn't a photographer in the free world who wouldn't at least consider his offer—except her.

''Not even for total autonomy?'' he asked levelly then leaned forward. ''Unrestricted artistic discretion? Unlimited expense account? And this for an annual salary?'' He pulled a notebook out of the breast pocket of his spanking-new bush shirt and scribbled down a figure. He ripped out the sheet of paper and slid it across the table in front of her.

When she saw the dollar figure, she couldn't help it. She gasped.

''You're not serious.''

''As a heart attack.''

Which is what he'd darned near given her. ''I don't get it. Why me?''

Web considered the woman sitting across from him sipping tea in her army fatigues. She'd cleaned herself up a bit, he noticed, which told him she must harbor a little female vanity beneath her commando appearance, after all. That and the promise of a dimple in her left cheek that he hadn't noticed before. He filed both bits of information away in case they came in useful later.

''Why you? Because you're good. I need good. It's that simple. And it's a helluva deal, Tonya,'' he pointed out.

When her frown deepened, he weighed his options.

How much did he tell her before he lost any advantage at all? His read on Tonya Griffin was that beneath that prickly exterior, she was straightforward, straight shooting and without pretense. In the game-playing department, she was clearly a novice. That didn't mean she couldn't see through a fake play and shoot him down if he tried to pull one. Going with his gut, he decided to tell her as much as he thought she needed to know.

"You'll not only be exclusive to Tyler-Lanier, you'll shoot exclusively for a new publication we hope to launch within six months, *Greater Outdoors*. Every issue will be filled with Tonya Griffin photos and nothing but Tonya Griffin photos."

That brought a full-fledged scowl to her face that, for some reason, melted him a little. She worked darn hard at looking stern. It really wasn't a good fit for her soft blue eyes and lacy lashes—not to mention lightly tanned skin that looked petal soft without its complement of mud on her flushed cheek.

"I still don't get it." Her finely arched eyebrows drew closer together. "I can think of a half-dozen photographers—all more experienced, all more skilled than I am—who could bring a lot more prestige to the magazine."

Okay. So she wasn't a prima donna, either, and that had him softening a little more and digging a little deeper to pull out the Tyler charm. "I don't want any other photographer. I want you. I don't need prestige from you, Tonya. Tyler-Lanier already has that. What I need is your viewpoint. I like the way you see things. I like the work you do. And that makes you my choice for the job.''

She rose then walked to the door and opened it. Stuffing her hands into her back pockets, she locked her knees and stared outside.

Her stance emphasized the slim length of her legs. The hands she'd shoved in her pockets pulled the fabric of her baggy shorts snug over her hips and left little detail of her curvy backside to the imagination. He felt a sharp kick of sexual awareness that shocked him.

She was a tomboy in olive drab, rough around the edges, tough as nails and not in his wildest dreams would she ever play the part in his romantic fantasies. At least he didn't want her to, and it bugged him more than a little that in the past hour or so he'd imagined more than one scenario involving him, her and some wild monkey love.

Cripes. It was crazy. He wasn't attracted to her. No way. If it weren't for C. C. Bozeman's insistence— C.C. just happened to be the major advertiser and therefore the major player in getting *Greater Outdoors* off the ground—that it was either Tonya Griffin or he pulled his advertising dollars, Web wouldn't be here making nice with this bullheaded little pixie anyway.

"Look," she said finally. "I'm flattered and I appreciate your situation, but I can't help you. I don't want to be tied to an exclusive contract." She looked back over her shoulder at him, resolve and just a little bit of regret clouding her eyes, before turning her attention back to the open door. "I'm sorry. But my answer is still no."

Then she walked outside and left him sitting and staring after her.

"Stubborn as a damn mule," he muttered under his breath.

Well, he'd dealt with mules before. His grandfather had been one of the biggest. It had always taken some time, but somehow Web managed to sway the old boy to his way of thinking.

He stared grimly at the door, kissing his midnight return to the city goodbye.

Okay. He could handle this until tomorrow. He'd make her see reason by then. He just had to figure out an angle that would make her come around. Everyone had a price; he didn't figure she was the exception. Although if the money he'd just offered and total creative freedom hadn't done the trick, he'd be damned if he knew what would.

He rose and walked out onto the stoop, scowled grimly. It was getting late. It had also cooled off several degrees as the sun was about to set and the wind had come up. A huge, black cloud bank was boiling in from the west. None of which sat too well with him. He'd had a helluva time finding his way here in daylight. Navigating his way back to International Falls through a rainstorm in the dark would be an even bigger disaster.

"So who knew I should have been a boy scout?" he muttered under his breath.

In the distance, near the food pans, a dozen or so

bears licked paws and backed up to trees to scratch. A little skirmish had broken out between two younger bears. The argument quickly ended when one of the older boars sent a low, warning growl their way.

They still looked hungry, he thought, not relishing the idea of walking the quarter mile in the dark back to where he'd parked his rented car—not after his encounter with Not-so-Gentle Ben. Not when there could be another full squadron of the critters skulking around in the woods looking for fresh meat and wondering if he had any more candy on him.

Speaking of hungry. He was starving. So were the mosquitoes. He swatted one off his neck. They were swarming now the darker it got. He squinted into the waning light. His reluctant hostess came tooling around a small shed, carrying an armload of firewood.

"You'd better get going." Head down, she trudged up the cabin steps past him. "You've got a two-hour drive and this being the last week of fishing season, you'll be lucky to find a room anywhere in town. And if those clouds break loose the road's going to be questionable and then some."

No way was he going to try to find his way back to town in the dark. "I passed several resorts on the way here."

"They'll be booked. Your best bet is back in the Falls."

His best bet was back in New York but thanks to her hardball tactics, he wasn't going to get within two thousand miles of Fifth Avenue today.

"Well," he said, as the first clap of thunder rumbled to the west and the wind gusted in an undeniable prelude to the fast-approaching storm, "if you're sure I can't talk you—"

"You can't," she assured him. "I'm sorry you went to so much trouble."

"Had to try," he said pleasantly. "Besides, it wasn't a total loss. Now I can say I've seen Minnesota. And that I almost got eaten by a bear."

She looked from him to the bears, seemed to consider, then reluctantly made an offer. "You want me to walk you back to your car?"

Male pride barely won out over his lily-livered, bear-fearing hide that yelled, *Hell, yes!* With effort, he sucked it up. "That's okay. I'll be fine." He was not going to cower behind Commando Cathy—even if it did afford him an unrestricted view of her butt.

She hesitated, then shrugged. "Right. Well. Suit yourself. Just stay on the path and you won't have any trouble with the locals."

She nodded toward the few bears still congregated around the food pans before she passed through the cabin door and kicked it shut behind her.

Thoughtful, Web stared down the quarter-mile path that led to the small parking area where he'd parked the rental, wondering what kind of reception he'd get when he showed up again tomorrow with a fresh set of arguments.

Thunder grumbled in the background, a clear threat this time. He looked up toward the darkening sky as the last bit of blue gave way to lead-gray clouds, heavy to bursting with rain. A fat raindrop hit him right between the eyes.

"Perfect," he muttered wearily, and headed down the path at a slow jog.

Three

After showering and slathering on lotion—a long overdue treatment for the skin she neglected more from thoughtlessness than design—Tonya slipped into a pair of fleecy-soft pink sweats and some warm socks. She'd just thrown some wood into the cast-iron stove to keep the chill at bay when lightning flashed through the windows of the tiny cabin.

Drying her hair with her damp bath towel, she counted out of habit. "One-one thousand, two-one thousand, thr—"

If the dishes hadn't already been chipped, the thunder rattling the cupboards before she finished her three count would have done the job.

"That hit close." She looked toward the roof and the sound of the rain pummeling the cabin. A metal shower stall was no place to be during a thunderstorm so she was glad she'd slipped in and out for a quick shampoo and scrub as soon as Web Tyler had left.

Rising on tiptoes, she reached the oil lamp sitting on top of a scarred pine bookcase loaded with Zane Grey westerns and some Farmer's Almanacs dating back to the 1930s. Charlie Erickson's reading selection was limited but well loved judging by the condition of the much-read paperbacks and magazines.

Instead of concerning herself with Web Tyler and worrying whether he'd made it back to the main highway before the storm hit, she wondered how Charlie was doing as rain peppered his log cabin like BBs. The wind—no longer rising, but full-out howling—battered the weathered logs, whipping the pine and ash into a frenzy of swaying, swishing limbs.

Needled branches clawed against the ancient structure. "An ancient structure that has stood strong against many, many storms," she assured herself aloud when the lights flickered, but the electricity miraculously stayed on.

She placed the lamp in the middle of the table and thought about Charlie, who had lived out here alone in this cabin for sixty of his eighty years, long before electric and telephone lines had been strung by the utility companies. He lived and loved the solitude, the wilderness and his precious bears. Bears he'd been luring onto his forty acres of timber with a supplemental diet of nuts and berries and dog food for six decades in the hopes of keeping them safe from hunters and poachers.

She'd called him at the hospital yesterday and assured him she was taking care of things, made him promise to rest and recuperate and follow doctors' orders. He'd been lucky to survive the heart attack three weeks ago, but, even at his age, full recovery was a possibility—if he stayed put and didn't rush things.

Speaking of rushing, torrents of water poured down the cedar-shake roof and gushed into overflowing eaves like a tidal flow. This wasn't the first storm she'd sat out since she'd arrived on the first of the month. Minnesota, she'd found, was a land of extremes. Extreme heat, extreme cold—sometimes, like today, all in the same day. It was also a land of extreme beauty. Extreme solitude was also a staple. Especially during a storm like this one.

She was glad Charlie was tucked safe and warm in his hospital bed in the Falls where an elderly volunteer by the name of Helga made special daily visits with rosy-cheeked smiles and lots of tender fussing.

"She's just a friend," Charlie had assured her when she'd visited him two days ago.

"If you say so, Charlie," she'd said, then laughed at his rheumy-eyed glare.

Another crack of thunder, as sharp as a whip, ricocheted through the cabin.

"Better safe than sorry," she told herself as she hunted around for a box of wooden matches in preparation for the power lines going down. She smiled when she found it and a candle as a bonus in the drawer next to the silverware. She'd just struck a match when the lights flickered again, then went out without so much as a lightning bolt to prompt them.

"And darkness fell with a whisper, not a bang," she reflected aloud, lifting the slim glass chimney off the lamp and setting flame to the wick. "And you're talking to yourself again, Griffin.

"Occupational hazard," she murmured and replaced the chimney, adjusting the wick so the cabin was pleasantly bathed in flickering light and dancing shadows. The faint fragrance of cherry-scented lamp oil blended with the smell of wet forest and her melon-and-floral shampoo. When you spent as much time alone as she did—either on remote photo shoots around the world or by choice during downtime—her own voice was the one she heard the most often.

Charlie had understood that. The old sweetheart was a lot like her. And a lot like his bears. He was a gruff docile bear of a man who lumbered about the land he loved and knew like the back of his hand. Like her, he was a loner and comfortable with it. Not that he was antisocial as some labeled her. He seemed to truly enjoy her company, had invited her into his home without hesitation when she'd arrived at his door with her camera equipment, her camping gear and a request to photograph his bears.

Another sizzle of lightning lit up the darkness like a strobe, the sharp report of thunder so loud and so close on its heels she jumped. She pressed her hand to her heart to stall the jackrabbit jumping around inside her chest.

"Holy cow," she finally managed to say on a

whoosh of a breath. "A tree probably went down with that strike."

For the heck of it, she picked up the phone. Just as she'd thought. It was dead. With miles of line cutting through acres and acres of timber, a branch or a fallen tree was always taking it out—often with a lot less provocation than a monster storm like this one.

Again, her thoughts involuntarily strayed to Web Tyler. For whatever reason, she didn't like to think of him caught in this deluge.

"He's a big boy. He can take care of himself."

At least he could in the city. Up here though, where the elements ruled and learning how to live with them made the difference, he was at a distinct disadvantage. She shook her head at the memory of how he'd looked, poster perfect, all turned out in his best *GQ* version of outdoor gear. But then, he could have been wearing a grungy T-shirt and holey jeans and one look at his hundred-dollar haircut and manicured nails would have shouted *city boy.*

One look had certainly shouted to her. And this time when her heart jumped, it wasn't because of the storm raging outside in the night.

For twelve years, she'd been convinced she'd gotten over her crush on him. Apparently, for twelve years she'd been fooling herself. And he didn't even remember her. If it wasn't so pathetic it would be laughable. She might have laughed because the irony was fitting, but just then the cabin door burst open, smacked against the wall and scared ten years off her life.

For the space of several hard, irregular heartbeats, all she could do was stand there, eyes wide, as a very wet, very angry man filled the cabin doorway like a hulking, misshapen monster out of a *Friday the 13th* movie.

The mud-splattered apparition—shouldering what she now recognized as a sodden duffel bag, not a grotesque Quasimodo-style hump—closed the door behind him with a muttered, "Yeah, I'd be happy as hell to come in out of the rain, thanks very much." She didn't know whether to laugh with relief that he wasn't an ax murderer or curse the gods of fate for sending Web Tyler back to her door.

Web had been seeing red for the better part of an hour. Now all he saw was pink. From her pink socks to her pink cheeks to her pink lips, Tonya the camo queen Griffin looked adorably pretty in pink, of all things. With her hair wet and flowing over her shoulders and down her back, she also looked soft and feminine and—hell.

He was wet and cold and way too relieved that he wasn't still wandering around out there in the biggest rain since Noah launched the ark to think about that now. He'd make sense of his reaction later, when his boots weren't full of sludge and his teeth weren't chattering like dice rolling across a craps table. And when his brain thawed out and saw her for what she really was—a problem he needed to solve.

Right now, however, he'd settle for some dry clothes and about a gallon of that herbal tea he'd choked down earlier. Anything to take the ice out of his blood.

"Are you all right?" she asked hesitantly.

"Considering that I'd just piled out of my stalled rental car when the tree fell on it, yeah, I guess you could say I'm just peachy."

"Oh my God."

He grunted then stiffened when a full-body shiver shook him. "Yeah. A lot of that going around."

Real concern mixed with the disbelief washing across her cheeks. "You're freezing. You need to get out of those clothes and into something dry."

He dropped his duffel and carry-on on the floor at his feet with a squishy thud. They both watched as water oozed from the soaked nylon bag. "Unless you've got something stowed away in a men's size large, I'm thinking dry may be as out of reach as warm."

"I'll come up with something," she said absently. "For now, get that shirt off."

From any other woman, he'd have taken the request as an invitation. From this woman, it was merely an order.

"What happened?" she added, his ice-cold fingers feeling stiff as screwdrivers and just as clumsy as he attempted to work the buttons free.

"Close as I can figure," he said as another chill eddied from the top of his head to the base of his spine, "the engine stalled when I hit a low spot in the road."

"How low?"

"Oh, about two feet under water low."

She muttered something under her breath—something about fools and flooded roads and stupidity and evidently seeing the difficulty he was having, she batted his fingers out of the way and started tackling his shirt buttons herself.

"Lot of that going around, too," he agreed around another shiver that had him clamping his jaw tight to keep the fillings from clattering out of his teeth. "I managed to snag my gear and bail out just before I heard this piercing crack, felt the earth tremble and knew something big was happening."

"Like a tree falling."

"On the car," he restated, suddenly far too aware that she was tugging on his shirttails and peeling his shirt off his shoulders.

"Big tree? Little tree?"

"Think sequoia."

She cut him a look.

"Okay, you stand on the ground looking up when a tree is heading toward you and see if you don't think the same thing. It was big. Big enough to smash that car like a pancake."

She froze. "Smashed? Is it drivable?"

"Drivable? Honey, it's not even visible."

Small fingers, soft and hot as firebrands against his frigid skin, hesitated, then skimmed his shoulder blade with unconscious sensuality as she turned him toward the light and examined his back.

"Ouch." He winced when she touched a tender spot.

"Looks like the tree didn't miss you entirely," she grumbled.

"I knew something got me. I didn't hang around long enough to figure out what."

"Over here," she ordered, every inch the drill sergeant, and pointed toward the chair she dragged away from the table.

"I'll get mud all over everything."

"We'll have the maid clean up in the morning," she said deadpan then ducked into the bathroom. She returned quickly with an armload of towels.

"It's a cabin," she pointed out when she saw he was still standing where she'd left him. "An old cabin and the floor has seen more than a little mud and water. Now get over here so I can look at your shoulder in the light."

Florence Nightingale, she was not. He toed off his boots and sodden socks and left both along with his shirt in a soggy pile by the door before walking stiffly across the few feet to the table.

Accepting the towel she offered, he buried his face in terry cloth then ran it roughly over his drenched hair while she lifted a glass oil lamp from the table and inspected his back.

"This hurt?" She probed his shoulder blade.

He shook his head again, trying to ignore the unexpected awareness of her hot hands on his bare back that had him shivering for any number of reasons that had nothing to do with how cold he was.

"How about here?"

"Ouch! Yes," he yelped when she probed harder.

"If that's the response you were looking for, then hell yes. It hurts like a bitch. Happy?"

"Marginally," she said, but her inspection turned gentle.

She leaned across him to set the lantern back on the table. The brush of her breasts against his back was accidental—warm and firm and much too provocative to miss, even if he felt like an icicle sitting there dripping on the floor.

She was all business as she lifted his arm, moving it this way and that, testing his extension and mobility.

"Just a bruise," she pronounced finally, releasing him. "A bad one, but nothing's broken."

He rolled a shoulder, testing it and stalling a wince. "Sorry to disappoint you."

She had nothing to say to that as she walked across the room again, reached into a cupboard and pulled down a Texas fifth of Canadian rye whiskey.

He could have wept with gratitude when she poured out three fingers and handed him the glass.

"This will take the ice out of the chill."

While he enjoyed the smooth burn of the liquor going down, she dug around in a bureau and finally came up with a stack of clothes.

"These are Charlie's." She handed him a heavy flannel shirt; a pair of soft, worn jeans and some thick, wool socks. "They'll be big on you, but they're dry and warm and that's what you need most right now. We need to get you warmed up and out of those wet pants before you get shocky. The bathroom's all yours.''

He was so stiff with wet and cold he felt as if he was eighty instead of thirty-five as he rose—he swore he heard his joints creaking—and shuffled on bare feet with blue toes toward the tiny bathroom.

He supposed there was something he should say. At a minimum, thanks and I'm sorry to intrude. But the fact was, his current frigid state aside, he was alert enough to realize this was an opportunity and was too busy thinking about how to take advantage of it to come up with anything else.

Now that he'd survived his first, and he hoped last, trial by Minnesota monsoon, he was in the exact position he needed to be to pull off this deal. He was bunkmates with Tonya Griffin—at least for the night. Granted, he would never have gone to such extremes to get an opportunity to talk with her again. Hell, he wasn't desperate enough to stage a near drowning and have his car crushed by a tree, but he could turn this into a plus. Lemons and lemonade and all that. A good businessman relied on luck as much as finesse. He wasn't about to discount an opportunity hand delivered on a silver platter—and he was a damn good businessman.

He was far from an expert on wilderness survival, but he didn't have to be related to a lumberjack to know that short of Paul Bunyan and Babe, his Blue Ox, showing up with their magic axes to clear it, the only road in was blocked but good. There wasn't much chance of anyone getting in or getting out of this particular parcel of timber tonight—maybe not even for the next few days. Which meant she'd be stuck with him for a while. Which meant he had a captive audience.

It was a prime opportunity to win her over. And now that he had the opportunity, he knew how to handle it from here. This was a game he knew how to play. If he couldn't talk one mule-headed, bear-loving, antisocial photographer into becoming rich and famous, then he'd throw in the towel.

"Here," she said from behind him as he was about to shut the bathroom door. When he turned, she handed him a lit candle. "You'll need this so you can see what you're doing."

He extended his hand and they both saw how badly it was shaking. Even with the help of the whiskey, he felt his bones had turned to ice cubes. Tonya reached past him and set the candle on the top of what appeared to be a small clothes hamper.

"Wish I could offer you a shower, but, like I said, with the power lines down the water pump doesn't work. I drew some water earlier anticipating the lights would go out. It'll just take a few minutes to heat a panful on the stove, and you can wash up a bit. The rain washed most of the mud off anyway."

With that, she shut the door.

And he was left standing in the flickering candle-light—and the surprising and arousing sight of a pair of pink lace panties and matching bra hanging from the shower-curtain rod.

Never in his wildest dreams would he have imagined that beneath her khaki-and-tan survivalists' clothes, Tonya Griffin liked the feel of lace against her skin. Or that he'd become aroused by the visuals her delicate lingerie conjured.

He couldn't stop himself. He reached out. Touched.

Damp. She'd evidently washed them out, then hung them to dry.

The shivering started again with a vengeance so he slowly shucked his soaked bush pants and tossed them on the floor of the shower stall. He was standing in nothing but his wet boxers, warming his hands over the candle, staring at those scraps of pink lace when he heard a soft tap on the door.

"Hot water," she announced.

When he opened the door, she was out of sight, but the panful of water sat on the floor.

He snatched it up greedily then actually laughed at the sweet anticipation of what appeared to be all of four miserly cups of hot water.

"Oh, how the mighty have fallen," he muttered, thinking of his plush apartment that came complete with a breathtaking view of the city skyline and a hot tub big enough to float a small battleship.

"Did you say something?" came from outside the door.

"Thanks," he said, dipping his frozen fingers in the water and groaning in appreciation.

"You're welcome."

"And you are toast, sweetheart," he murmured so she couldn't hear. As he stared at the delicious sight of her undies, he felt only a faint stirring of guilt over the plan that he was slowly formulating. He had to get her to sign on the dotted line.

But why guilt? In the long run, he would actually be doing her a favor. First, there was the sweet deal he was offering. Second, how long had it been, he wondered, since a man made her feel like anything other than a commodity? How long had it been since a man had told her she was pretty and vital, as well as talented?

"A long time if her thorny disposition is any indication," he muttered aloud.

Past time, he decided and dipped a washcloth into the water while it still retained some heat. Sometime between now and when he left here, he was going to soften up the hard case with the tangled blond braid and lake-blue eyes. He was going to be attentive and interested in her work and let her know he was interested in her, too. Just a little harmless flirting. Just a little playful teasing to remind her she was more than a reclusive photographer.

She was a woman. She needed to be reminded of that. A woman with a woman's wants and a woman's needs and a woman's weaknesses—for lace and a little candlelight, and a man's interest. And he knew full well how to exploit those weaknesses.

When the dust settled, she'd feel better about herself. He'd get his contract. No one would get hurt.

Still as cold as frost on a windowpane, he shrugged into the shirt. As she'd said, it was a little big. Okay, it was *huge,* but the worn flannel felt soft and warm against his skin. So did the socks.

He was standing with his back to the shower stall, eyeballing the jeans when something hit him on the head. He reached up and came away with a skimpy handful of damp, pink lace panties.

He couldn't help it—he was a man after all—he rubbed the panties between his fingers, enjoying the feel of the sensuous fabric in his hand before bringing them to his face and inhaling the floral scent of soap and woman.

For the first time since he'd stepped out of the rain, he felt a real flush of warmth slide through his blood.

Tonya was stirring a pot of leftover chicken soup on the gas stove when she heard the bathroom door open and close.

It was ridiculous, but she'd been wavering between stoic fatalism and gross embarrassment ever since she'd remembered she'd washed out her underwear and hung them over the curtain rod.

Big deal. So she wore pink panties. And sometimes red or blue or peach, or if the mood struck her, black. He's seen women's underwear before, probably taken off his fair share. It was nothing to get bent out of shape over that he'd seen hers.

So why did it feel so intimate? Because she'd practically undressed him just now. Because she'd seen his bare, broad shoulders, the solid musculature of his chest, felt his skin beneath her fingers.

And because twelve years ago, he'd been the source of her biggest crush. Because he still had the ability to make her pathetic heart go all atwitter. And he didn't even remember her.

She was such a loser.

When she heard him cross the room to the wood-stove, she felt the tips of her ears flame hot with embarrassment. She sucked in a deep breath and tried to come up with something to say. He beat her to it.

"So who's Charlie? And is he related to the Incredible Hulk?"

Still stirring the soup, she glanced over her shoulder. And couldn't help but smile. "Feeling a bit like you're playing the lead in *Who Shrunk the Publisher*?"

He actually chuckled as he looked down at himself. He'd rolled the sleeves of the shirt up a couple of times and had bunched the waistband of the jeans in one fist to hold them up. He'd also rolled the cuffs of the jeans but they still broke across the arches of his feet and dragged on the floor.

He was thirty-five years old and one of the most powerful men in the international publishing world, but right now he looked like a little boy lost in his daddy's duds.

She turned down the heat on the soup and set the spoon in a trivet. "I'll get you something to hold up those pants."

Crossing to a dresser, she rifled around a bit and found a belt and a pair of red-and-blue-striped suspenders. Sheer orneriness made her opt for the suspenders.

"Here you go."

He took them with a *you've got to be kidding* look. "Well, just hand me an ax or a chainsaw. I'm an outdoorsman now."

"Not quite," she assured him, forgoing a threatening smile for a bland look.

"Right. Clothes don't make the man."

Oh, but they did, she thought, remembering the first time she'd seen him in one of his Savile Row suits. She'd taken a tumble right then and there.

"Hungry?" she asked, steering away from the memory.

"Oh, God. You're going to feed me, too? Can I buy you a small country or something?"

"Definitely hungry." This time her grin won out. "Sit. If you're still chilled, grab that comforter off the rocker and wrap it around your shoulders."

"I'm much better. Thanks. For a while there it was Popsicle city. Can't remember the last time I was so cold."

"Do you drink milk?"

"Absolutely. Good Lord, that smells like heaven." He walked up behind her and inhaled deeply and appreciatively.

She did a little deep, appreciative inhaling, too. A woman fresh from a shower smelled like flowers and citrus. A man fresh from a shower smelled like a man. This man, fresh from a rain shower, smelled clean and strong and so male it made her throat ache.

It had been way too long since her senses had been assaulted this way. So long, her hands were a little shaky as she set the spoon aside and turned off the flame under the soup.

"It's pretty standard-issue chicken soup," she assured him, moving out of breathing distance of all those enticing scents, and searched out a bowl in the cupboard. "Not exactly the haute cuisine you're used to in the city."

"Okay, let's get something straight." He placed his hands on her shoulders and turned her around to face him. "What I'm not used to is fending off hungry bears, negotiating flooded roads, dodging falling trees and searching for shelter in a storm. And, believe it or not, I'm not used to imposing myself on someone uninvited. Especially when she clearly doesn't appreciate my unexpected company but still dries me off, warms me up and feeds me anyway.

"Tonya," he added, giving her shoulders a little squeeze, "do you honestly think that after everything you've done for me I'm going to gripe about the food? Food that not only smells great but like something I remember from my mom's kitchen?"

His eyes were dark in the limited light of the oil lamp and the candle flame he'd brought with him out of the bathroom. His expression was sincere. She stared at him for a moment in stupefied silence as he smiled down at her with the kindest, most benevolent, amused look on his face. Whatever moment's easiness she'd felt over the earnest entreaty in his words flipped off as the power had flipped off earlier.

Every muscle in her body stiffened. She'd seen that look before. It had been many years ago. Twelve years, to be precise. It had been the night of the Tyler-Lanier Christmas party, and she had been in the back seat of a cab with him. He'd offered to take her home from the party. It had been the equivalent of the prince courting the peasant girl. That kind of thing didn't happen to Tonya, who had always felt she looked like a tomboy trying to play dress up. Regardless, she'd been high on the rush of attention and a little dreamy-eyed. The fact that he'd kept calling her Tammy had been only mildly annoying in the face of his attention. Besides, she'd had just enough holiday champagne that she'd seen his offer and the moment as her slim window of opportunity to take her crush to the next level.

Seduced by his smiles, she'd thrown herself into his arms in the back seat of the taxi and surprised them both by kissing him.

Bold as brass. Out of the blue.

It had been wonderful. Everything she'd dreamed of as his kiss had lit her up like the Rockefeller Center Christmas tree.

Until he'd ended it—and her euphoria. The look on his face when he'd eased her arms from around his neck was the same look he was giving her now. Kind. Benevolent. Amused.

Four

"**Y**ou asked about Charlie," Tonya said abruptly, as much to diffuse the memory of that long-ago Christmas blunder as to tone down the intensity of the moment. She turned back to the pan of soup. Her hand was still shaking as she ladled out a generous helping then shoved the bowl into his hands. "This is Charlie Erickson's cabin. The bears are Charlie's, too."

She listened to the soft sound of his stocking feet hitting the floor as he walked toward the table while the wind continued to batter and the rain showed no sign of letting up.

"The bears are Charlie's?"

She set a glass of milk, a tin of crackers and a soupspoon in front of him. "In a manner of speaking. He's lived out here for sixty years and has been supplementing their natural food with nuts, berries, dog food and anything else he can beg off grocers and restaurant owners. Of the approximately one hundred fifty bears in Koochiching County, forty to sixty of them know Charlie's forty acres offers safe haven, and they congregate here morning and night.''

He downed a healthy spoonful of soup. ''Safe haven?''

''From hunters. Hunting season is due to open next week so he'd been beefing up their meals in the hopes of luring more out of harm's way. You would have seen the No Hunting signs posted on your drive in.''

He nodded and chased the soup with a long swallow of milk.

She tried not to appreciate the fact that he ate like a man, not some pampered urbanite, too genteel to dig in and enjoy.

''So where's Charlie now?''

''Recovering from a heart attack in the hospital in International Falls.''

His spoon stopped midway to his mouth. ''That's a tough one.''

She fussed with a dishcloth, tidying up around the stove. ''For an eighty-year-old man, he's doing well, though. It's been two weeks since the attack. The damage was actually minimal. Another week or two and he should be able to come home.''

He propped an elbow on the table and considered her. ''And you plan on staying and taking care of his bears until he's able.''

She shrugged. "Only seems right since he was gracious enough to let me photograph them."

After another long look, he went back to his soup. But for the sounds of the storm, silence filled the one-room cabin as he ate. The darkness and the storm effectively cocooned them from the rest of the world—but not from her thoughts.

Tonya had arrived in New York City from Manchester, Iowa—small-town U.S.A.—a gung-ho nineteen-year-old with an Associate's Degree from the local community college, a fistful of dreams and a raw talent in need of development. Her first job had been as a photographer's assistant at Tyler-Lanier Publishing Group. It had also been her last in the city. Some had called it downsizing. Tonya, who had harbored hopes that the entry-level job would help her toward bigger and better things, had called it the "Knife before Christmas." She'd been handed her pink slip on Christmas Eve day—the day after the Christmas party. The day after she'd made a colossal fool of herself by throwing herself at Web.

"How did you hear about this place?" Web's deep voice wrenched her back to the moment and away from her woolgathering.

"How does a photographer ever hear about a potential shoot? Other photographers. The Jesups and I were on an assignment for *Outdoor Life*," she said, referring to the renowned husband-and-wife camera team who had taken her under their wing several years ago and shown her the ropes.

"They told me about how they'd done a spread on

the bears for *Parade Magazine* thirty or so years ago. They'd never forgotten Charlie. Or Minnesota or the bears and they talked about the experience with such affection I decided I wanted to see it for myself.''

She brought the soup pan over to the table and refilled his bowl. ''When I finished my shoot in the outback last month, I had some time to kill and decided to spend it here.''

''And now you know what intrigued the Jesups.''

She looked at him, pleased in spite of herself that he understood. ''Now I know.''

''And is it worth it?'' He propped his elbows on the table again, the glass of milk cupped in his hands.

She couldn't help but notice his hands. They weren't a working man's hands, but they were strong hands, heavily veined, the fingers long. An uninvited visual of those fingers trailing over her skin, touching her in the most intimate places sent a flush to the tips of her ears again.

She quickly looked away, lifted the curtain from the window on the pretense of looking outside. It was pitch black now and the only thing visible was the sheet of rain blasting against the aged windowpane. ''Is what worth it? Photographing the bears?''

''The solitary life. The nomadic existence. Don't you ever miss the city?''

She dropped the curtain and, because she felt this constant need to do something around him, she walked back to the woodstove and fiddled with the flue. She didn't like it that he might have hit on something that had been working on her lately. She did lead a solitary life. And sometimes it was lonely.

"I grew up in a town of less than ten thousand people. So the city—any city—has never been a pulse beat for me," she hedged, rather than admit to those feelings.

"It's every beat for me." Leaning back, he balanced on the rear chair legs. "I'd go stir-crazy out here for any length of time."

"Well—" she glanced from the woodstove to him "—you might just get the chance to put that to the test."

"Yeah." He let the chair come to rest on all four legs. "I figured that when the tree went down. Actually, I figured if I lived until morning, I might just find myself stuck out here for a few days. The road is completely blocked."

"Ever run a Bobcat?"

He pushed out a laugh. "Those are little tractorlike things, right?"

She shot him a patently patient look. "Yeah. Those are little tractorlike things."

"I've seen ads for them in our magazines. Does that count? No? Well, won't a road crew or something be out to clear things up?"

"The county doesn't maintain this road. Charlie does. Or his neighbors do when they get themselves dug out."

"Neighbors?" He dug back into his soup.

"Don't get your hopes up. The closest one is about five miles due south."

"So, you're saying you're stuck with me for a while."

"It would seem so, yes."

"I really am sorry about this."

"Yeah, well, if you don't get cabin fever on me, we've got enough food to last for a week or so, and water is never a problem near a lake."

"There's a lake here, too?"

She did a double take, blinked. "Hel-lo. This is Minnesota? Land of ten thousand lakes?"

"Oh, yeah. Where the men smell like fish and look like bears, right?"

A laugh escaped before she could stall it. She'd often thought the same thing herself of some of the rough-and-tumble and kindhearted north-woods types who spent all their time fishing and hunting and rarely saw a razor or a bar of soap. "Well, some of them at any rate."

"And what do you do here at night?" His gaze slowly scanned the cabin. "I mean, besides bounce off the walls with boredom?"

"I read. I develop my film. There are several jig-saw puzzles stacked in the bookcase."

"And?"

She lifted a shoulder, feeling a little defensive. "And that's about it."

"What more could a man ask for."

"Now say that like you mean it."

"Not in this lifetime." He stood, stretched, then started prowling around the cabin. "I suppose e-mail would be too much to hope for."

She didn't even bother to answer.

"That's what I thought."

She tried to ignore him as, restless, he wandered around, touching this, picking up that, warming his hands again on the stove. But ignoring roughly six feet of gorgeous male was a tough trick in a twenty-by-twenty room with no TV, no radio and no way out.

"You might want to get some of your clothes out of your duffel and hang them up to dry," she suggested, because he wasn't going to be content to wade around in Charlie's clothes for too long. "I've strung a drying line in the corner."

It was a little sad to watch him fumble around with the wet clothes and hang them clumsily with clothespins and on hangers—he no doubt had maids that normally did that for him—but no way was she touching his personal things. It was just too…*personal.* And she wasn't anyone's maid. She did, however, move his boots over by the woodstove so the heat would help dry the leather.

"Got any cards?" he asked when he'd done his best—or his worst as the case may be.

"Actually, I think there are some." She dug around in a drawer and finally came up with a ragged deck. She tossed them on the table. "Knock yourself out."

"If I had a hammer, I'd give it a try."

She turned her back to hide her smile. "Think of this as an opportunity to get in touch with your inner self."

He grunted as he sat and picked up the deck. "Now there's a scary thought."

"Usually is," she agreed and washed the few dishes from their dinner—she'd eaten earlier—while he shuffled the cards.

"How about a little gin?"

"Sorry. Charlie only stocks whiskey."

"And damn fine whiskey, too. But I meant gin rummy. You could make a small fortune. I'm as good at cards as I am at this outdoor survival business."

"Well, in that case I'll pass. It wouldn't be fair to take advantage of you."

He just smiled and kept on shuffling. "Is solitaire six rows or seven?"

"Seven."

"Somehow, I knew you'd know."

For some reason, his statement and the way he said it sounded like a slur. "Meaning?"

He looked up, considered her expression and held his hands up on either side of his head in an *I surrender* pose. "Meaning nothing. Except that I understand you spend a lot of time alone on your shoots, so I figured you probably get bored sometimes. Solitaire is the universal boredom cure, right?"

She considered his statement and picking up the poker, stirred the wood in the cast-iron stove.

"Hey, really. I didn't mean anything by it. And just out of curiosity, what did you think I meant?"

That she was such poor company no one wanted to be around her, that's what she'd thought. That stuck with her and a deck of cards, a man would opt for the cards rather than her company, in or out of bed, that's what she'd thought.

My God, where was this coming from and why was she feeling so defensive? So she'd had a couple of disastrous relationships, and yeah, they'd shaken her confidence in herself as a woman.

She'd been driven to succeed after her failure in New York. Her love life had suffered in the process. The two semiserious relationships she'd been involved in since had eventually drifted off into nothingness. Her extended photo shoots often took her out of the state, even out of the country for long periods of time. It was a little difficult to cultivate intimacy long distance, and while she welcomed the idea of a special someone, she hadn't met the man who was willing to take a back seat to her career or accept the way she made her living. And then, there was always her little fantasy about Web. She'd never quite been able to let go of her fascination with him.

In spite of it, life was good, even if her work pretty much precluded the opportunity to find someone to share it with. She'd put her failure in New York behind and had gotten on with her life. But she'd thought of Web Tyler a little too often, with a little too much remorse along the way.

Now, suddenly, he was here and she was questioning herself all over again just because he'd shown up out of the blue in gorgeous living color. Her single biggest professional defeat and one of her more embarrassing personal moments were wrapped up in this man, and all he had to do was make an appearance and she was fighting with everything in her not to react to him like that unsophisticated, naive nineteen-year-old again. Darn her stupid, bug-bitten hide, she'd never forgotten him or that kiss. However, there wasn't a spark of recognition on his face—of course—she'd been twenty pounds heavier then. She'd also worn glasses and her hair had been short and spiked. But still…

Disgusted, she tossed another log on the fire and stood, dusting her hands on her sweats. The man was just making conversation. He was bored. And she was being surly. And her extended silence had him looking at her as if she'd just landed in a spaceship.

"Gin, you said?" She pulled out a chair and sat down across from him as much to prove to herself she could handle this like an adult as to appease him.

He looked surprised and then he smiled—kind of a pleased, playful smile that had her lips twitching just a little bit.

"I'll warn you now, I'm a poor loser."

She didn't doubt it for a minute. "That'll work out just fine because I'm a really obnoxious winner."

He slid the cards in front of her. "Cut?"

"Just deal."

"How many points are you going to spot me?"

She watched his hands, sure and expert, deal the cards out one by one and wondered just how bad he was planning on scamming her. "This isn't golf, Tyler. You don't get a handicap."

"Ah. So you're one of those."

She studied her hand as he picked up his cards and arranged them. "One of those what?"

"A hardnose."

"Because I'm not going to give you an edge?"

He grinned. "Because as gorgeous as you are, you've got a cutthroat look about you. You're going to beat up on me real bad, aren't you?"

"Only if you cheat." But he was cheating already, trying to distract her with pretty words. *Gorgeous.* Now there was a word she had never associated with herself and she seriously doubted that he did, either.

"I might push the envelope a little sometimes, but cheat? Never." Pure devilry lit his eyes and made it clear he'd pull out all his dirty tricks if the stakes were high enough. She was going to have to watch herself very carefully around him.

His eyes brightened as she drew a card then discarded it. He snatched up the card she threw away with barely suppressed glee.

She couldn't help it. She laughed. "You know, for a businessman, you don't have much of a poker face."

"Good thing this is gin then and not poker. Besides, this isn't business." He gave her an *are you sure you want that* look when she scooped up his discard. "This is pleasure. Pure pleasure," he added in a voice that snapped her gaze to his, but not before she'd let it dart to the bed.

Oh, God. He'd caught it. Of course he had. His eyes were suddenly alight with curiosity and speculation, which proved he didn't miss a thing. And she needed to marshal her words, actions and thoughts around this man or she was going to embarrass herself in any number of humiliating ways before she got rid of him.

"Are you going to draw or what?" she snapped, angry with herself and taking it out on him.

"Impatient, too," he observed conversationally, then he winked at her. "I like that in a woman."

Before she could even gather her thoughts to decide if he'd meant anything sexual by his remark, he very calmly laid down his entire hand and tossed away his discard. "Gin."

Her mouth fell open. "No way. Not this soon."

Again he smiled, and while she'd like to think so, there was nothing sinister in it. "Maybe next time you should cut them."

While she was skeptical about everything from his quick win to his flirting—and he was definitely flirting, at least a little bit—she quietly counted her points and jotted them down. "Maybe next time I will."

And maybe the next time he asked her to entertain him, she'd go with her gut instinct and tell him no, instead of taking pity on the poor misfit urbanite who should look ridiculous in giant sized flannel and lumberjack dungarees. He *should* look ridiculous but, unfortunately for her, he looked like exactly what he was. Gorgeous…a word that definitely applied to him. He also looked self-assured, at ease and hunky.

Something about the quiet, the dark and the isolation also made him look just a little dangerous. Not in a "physical harm" sort of way, but in a "break

her heart'' sort of way. And she just wasn't going to
let that happen again. She'd had just a little too much
experience in that area—which is why she preferred
solitude.

"Let's make this more interesting," he suggested
as she dealt out seven cards then laid the deck on the
table between them and turned a card face up.

When she met his gaze, there was so much heat in
his eyes that dozens of interesting stakes came to
mind. She was disgusted with herself for even thinking them.

"How about a penny a point?"

His eyebrows rose. "Whoa, that's a little rich for
my blood."

"Right. Like your blood couldn't buy my blood
and have enough left over to feed every mosquito in
Minnesota for the next millennium."

He chuckled. "Well—"

"And if you mention exclusive contract, the
game's over."

His guilty look told her that's exactly what he'd
had in mind although he denied it.

"Never crossed my mind."

"Uh-huh. Then what did?"

"How about if I win, I get to tag along with you
tomorrow when you work?"

She folded her cards and stared at him, not bothering to mask her suspicion. "My work involves
tracking through the woods filming bears. There are
icky things like dirt and mud and bugs and aching
muscles involved."

"Admittedly, that sounds like more fun than I'm equipped to handle but I'm willing to give it a go."

She shook her head. "Why?"

He lifted a shoulder. "Curiosity, I guess."

"Curiosity? About the bears?"

"That, too. But I'm more interested in why a beautiful, intelligent woman prefers to spend her time— *all* of her time from what I hear—skulking around forests and enduring jungle heat and frigid mountain ranges, not to mention snake-infested Amazon rivers and sand fleas in the desert, when she could have a cushy life in the city photographing temperamental models in air-conditioned studios with several thousand of the best restaurants in the world a cab ride away."

Tonya hadn't heard much after beautiful, intelligent woman. This on top of the gorgeous reference.

There were two possible reasons why Web was saying these things. Either he thought she was beautiful and intelligent, or he wanted to make her *think* he thought she was beautiful and intelligent. The first possibility shouldn't matter. But it did. Too much if the flush of heat she felt creeping up her face was an indicator.

The second possibility seemed more plausible, though less thrilling. Which begged the question: why?

What was he up to?

Maybe he still thought he could charm her into signing his precious contract. Maybe he thought sweet-talking her was the way to get it done.

Did she look that desperate for compliments? Further, did she look like the kind of woman who needed them? Or was that simply the way he was used to dealing with women in his business?

No. He was too smart for that. Most of the women she knew were also too smart to fall for such an obvious ploy.

So what was he up to?

Maybe he really was curious about the bears and felt a little embarrassed about expressing enthusiasm. A man who had traveled and seen as much as he had would be expected to be fairly urbane regarding something as unsophisticated as black bears.

The idea that he actually thought she was beautiful was too far-fetched to consider—and yet she did. That bothered her almost as much as his words.

"You want to go on a shoot? No problem. I'll take you along tomorrow, win or lose."

"Then what will we play for?"

There was way too much mischief in his smirk. So much, she decided then and there to show no mercy the rest of the game. "Loser carries the photo equipment and supplies."

"Deal."

"Just so you know, I'm going to whip your ass, Tyler."

His smile said he liked her sass. "Do your worst, Griffin. Don't forget, you've got a little hole to dig yourself out of."

Little holes were no problem. It was the big ones, the ones you had to claw and crawl your way out of, that she tended to avoid. She was not going to fall into a big hole over Web Tyler.

No matter that he'd called her beautiful and intelligent. And gorgeous.

No matter that he looked relaxed and playful and unexpectedly comfortable in Charlie's big shirt as he pushed himself up on the back legs of the chair and contemplated his cards.

No matter that she kept envisioning the two of them buried under the covers of Charlie's lumpy old bed while the rusty springs squeaked out a happy little chorus and she made a little noise of her own.

She wasn't even aware that she was staring at the bed when she heard him clear his throat.

"You going to play or what?" he asked, mimicking her earlier impatience.

What was definitely the word of the day. What bad luck had let him find her? What had God had in mind for her when he'd dropped that tree on his car? And what was it going to take to get her head back on straight and back to business?

She'd made minced meat out of him. Beat him three out of three games. And she'd been a better winner than he'd been a loser, crying foul just to get her going.

Against all odds and his throbbing shoulder, Web grinned in the dark as he lay in her sleeping bag in front of the woodstove. If she'd had her way, she'd be the one bedded down on the floor and he'd be the one in the bed.

"Don't make me play the macho card," he'd told her with a stern but totally staged scowl. "I'm the man. You're the woman. That makes you the softer, weaker sex. It's my job to sleep on the hard ground then hunt up a moose or caribou for breakfast while you gather wood and chew on deer hide—or something equally primitive and earthy."

He was getting used to her droll looks, like the one she'd shot him then.

"So, I have to put up with this trash talk because I beat you?" she'd asked as she unrolled the down-filled nylon bag in front of the fire.

"You have to put up with it because, while I was in the bathroom, you snuck out in the rain to get your sleeping bag out of the shed when I'd told you to wait and I'd get it for you."

"You don't have any dry boots," she'd pointed out. "I do. Plus I have rain gear. Being a member of the weaker sex, I think of things like that."

"You will *not* sleep on the floor," he'd insisted.

Whether she had simply decided not to argue with him or whether she saw by the look in his eyes that he meant business, she'd given in without further fuss. "Fine. It's all yours."

She'd disappeared into the bathroom then emerged a few minutes later looking all of sixteen-years-old in the oversize faded red sleep shirt he'd noticed hanging on a hook on the back of the bathroom door. He'd been too occupied with her lace panties hung up to dry; he hadn't given the T-shirt much thought before.

She dove straight for the bed with a request for

him to toss another log on the fire then put out the lamp before he turned in. She'd pulled the covers up to her chin and that had been that.

Over an hour had passed since. Outside, the worst of the thunder boomers appeared to be over. The rain had let up a little and the wind had calmed down by a few knots. Inside, however, an electrical charge hovered on the night air and rivaled the light show the storm had put on at its apex. If he was being honest with himself, the storm had as much to do with the sexual awareness layering the breathing room in the tiny cabin as it did with the absolute absurdity of his present situation.

Web Tyler, mover, shaker, top dog in one of the most affluent and prestigious publishing conglomerates in the free world, a man who dated celebrities, who dined with kings and slept in palaces, was bunked out on the floor of a drafty cabin like a damn camp counselor. In a pair of super-jumbo-size gray sweatpants roomy enough for two—and all he could think about was getting Tonya, the camp director, into the pants with him. Or at least out of hers.

Could he get any more sophomoric?

It didn't help, either, that he was pretty sure he wasn't the only one still awake. Goldilocks of the sixty bears was a little unsettled herself if the recurrent creak of what must be an ancient set of bed springs was any indication. Not one yawn; not one soft snuffling little snore; not one deep, even breath had come from the direction of the old bed since she'd plopped her sexy little body down.

And she did have a sexy little body. The lantern light couldn't generate enough candlepower to reach the farthest corner of the cabin, but it didn't take much light to define the gentle outline of a woman's silhouette beneath a sleep shirt worn thin with age and washing. One unplanned but well-timed look in her direction and he'd caught a glimpse of the lush curves beneath said same shirt as she'd crossed the room and turned back the covers.

He rolled to his back, suppressed a groan as the bruise on his shoulder complained and crossed his arms beneath his head. The movement rustled the nylon and down and stirred up the scent he'd been trying to ignore every bit as much as the image of her generous breasts pressed in relief against the translucent T-shirt.

The sleeping bag smelled of her. Softly feminine. Faintly flowery. Enticingly erotic. A little like mosquito spray.

He stalled a laugh at the idea he'd get turned on by bug spray.

One more time, boys and girls. Sophomore stuff.

He stared at the dancing shadows the light from the stove cast on the peaked ceiling. He didn't get it.

For the hundredth time, she was not his type. And she was not on the market. For that matter, neither was he. He was too busy to initiate a romantic relationship. Which she would never agree to anyway.

For the last time, Tonya was merely a business proposition. Granted, he'd decided to play to her female vanity as a means to an end, but that's as far as it went.

The bed creaked again. He couldn't help it. He turned his head toward her. Watched as she rolled to her side facing the wall and away from him. Her hair, which had dried in a soft tangle of curls spilling halfway down her back, made him think of angel hair. Luxurious as silk, it spread across her pillow like a tumble of flax ribbons.

The gentle curve of her hip made an enticing and provocative little hill beneath the old patchwork comforter, the valley of her small waist an intriguing contrast. Just like her transformation from khakis and camouflage to pink lace panties had taken away all the hard edges, it also lent her vulnerability.

You're not as tough as you want me to think you are, are you darlin'? And you're not nearly as indifferent to me as you want me to think you are, either.

But he had no business going there.

No true interest, either, he assured himself as he rolled away from her and faced the opposite wall. It was just the circumstances, the boredom, the infernal silence. And the necessity of getting her to sign his contract and getting on his way.

So why was he smiling as he lay there listening to her deep sigh? Damned if he knew. He wasn't cut out for this—this back-to-basics wilderness experience, or the isolation. And yet, once he'd thawed out and gotten his belly full, he'd actually enjoyed himself tonight. He'd relaxed. For the first time since—hell, he couldn't remember when. Go figure.

He'd also found a sense of humor he'd forgotten he had, he hadn't pulled it out of the bag for so long. In a cabin in the woods, with no electricity, no cabs speeding down the streets outside—no *streets*—no sirens wailing, no Broadway marquees blinking. Even the phone was out and he'd lost his cell somewhere during the course of his near-death experience with the tree.

And yeah. He'd still enjoyed himself. Playing cards with Tonya Griffin, who'd gotten just a little too much pleasure out of *whipping his ass,* as she'd put it in such earthy terms.

Earthy. There was that word again. It suited her. She was real, enduring, sustaining and, if the lush fullness of her breasts and the sweet curve of her hip were any indication, fertile.

Go to sleep, he ordered himself.

Think about tomorrow. He willed his muscles to grow because, in the morning, he was going to play pack mule and he strongly suspected she wouldn't go easy on him.

Hell of a deal.

So why was he still grinning when he finally fell asleep? And why did he feel so at peace and so comfortable with himself on a floor as hard as a New York city street?

Five

When Tonya opened the cabin door, the morning sky was pure blue and as clear as the night had been ink-black and shrouded in clouds. She slipped silently outside so as not to wake up her *guest*.

Birdsong greeted her like the soft tinkle of wind chimes as she descended the wet wooden steps. Chickadees and nuthatches chirped like gossiping old men around the feeders she kept filled with safflower and sunflower seeds. Two hummingbirds buzzed by so close she could feel the flutter of their wings then they stopped on a dime at the feeder that was getting a little low on sugar water.

"Whoa! What the heck was that?"

She spun around to see Web standing in his stocking feet on the top step. He'd thrown on Charlie's flannel shirt. It hung open over his bare chest. The gray sweatpants she'd dug up for him to sleep in appeared to be sliding south on his lean hips by slow degrees. All in all she saw way too much tanned skin, way too much soft silky hair covering a chest and abs that could have sold anything from gym memberships to designer underwear.

He had way too much sex appeal. Everything about him had her blood running hot.

She quickly turned back to watch the hummingbirds while her heart fluttered about the same speed as their frantically beating little wings. Good Lord, the man was potent.

He shouldn't look so good. He should look like a sad sack in Charlie's size XXXL clothes. He had a bad case of bed head, creases on his stubbled cheek from his pillow and his eyes were still a little bleary. But he was also all man, all male. And primitively sexual against the backdrop of the forest and the weathered cabin with the crisp September morning air puckering his nipples into tight little buttons.

Unfortunately, he was the reason she'd spent a sleepless night tossing and turning in Charlie's bed. He had invaded her private domain and stirred up all these feelings she'd managed to keep under wraps for so long.

"Hummingbirds," she finally said, trying to regain her equilibrium. "Rubythroats. By rights, I should have taken their feeders down by now. This time of year they should begin their southward migration." She shrugged. "Haven't been able to make myself do it. They're so incredible. I love watching them flit from flower to feeder and chase each other like mini Blackhawks then disappear into the pine boughs.''

She would miss a lot of things about Charlie's woods when she finally left here. The pleasures had been many. The surprises endless. But it wasn't the thought of leaving the woods that had her babbling like an idiot. It was an effort to avoid looking at Web's chest. Or his abs. Or at the way his mouth was softly swollen from sleep. Even the night's growth of beard was sexy; it made him look like a bad boy and she wondered just how bad he could be if he set his mind to it.

He yawned and rubbed sleep from his eyes. How nice that *one* of them had slept. She let out a breath through puffed cheeks. She'd pay for her sleeplessness today. She'd already decided he was going to pay for it, too, just as soon as she fed the bears milling around at the edge of the clearing.

''Looks like the breakfast crowd is starting to arrive,'' he said from behind her.

''Oh, they've been here a while. Patiently waiting.''

A big bear stood on his hind legs and growled toward her general direction.

''Your definition of patience and mine would seem to fall at opposite ends of the scale. You aren't really going out there among them, are you?''

''We have an understanding,'' she assured him and headed into the shed for food. ''I feed them and they don't eat me. Works well. You, however, should stay put.''

"If you insist.''

She grinned. She knew he wasn't about to take so much as a baby step off the porch as long as the bears were in the neighborhood.

"Hungry, huh, kids?'' she said aloud when she caught sight of twin bear cubs in the tree. She made a clicking sound with her teeth that she'd heard their mother make. "That's Jenna and Barbara Bush… no…look higher. There, about halfway up that lodgepole pine. They're Laura's spring cubs. She sent them up there until she gives the all clear that it's safe.''

"Guess that answers one of my questions.''

"Which is?''

"Which is, no, I didn't miss out on an opportunity to save myself from becoming bear bait just because I never got around to learning how to climb a tree when I was a kid.''

She hid her smile by setting a bucket on the ground and pouring Charlie's food mixture into it. "See the big guys staked out around the perimeter? That would be Eisenhower and Nixon. The one with the scar on his snout is Agnew. They're three of the older boars.''

"I'm starting to see a pattern here. Charlie wouldn't happen to be a staunch Republican, would he?''

Again, she grinned. "And damn proud of it. Ah, there's Bush I, Bush II and Cheney.''

He grunted out a chuckle. "It's beginning to sound

like a political convention, at the very least a caucus. So why are the others hanging back? Is there a Clinton loyalist lurking about somewhere?''

''No one eats until the elder boars give the okay. I don't know what the signal is but rest assured, the bears do.''

She walked away, filled the food pans then repeated the process, setting more buckets of food on several tree stumps, at the base of a number of large boulders, even in some scarred feeding boxes Charlie had made from a downed cedar.

''They are magnificent creatures, aren't they?'' he said as she approached the shed to lock it up tight.

Speaking of magnificent creatures. Every time she looked at him she found something else that fascinated her. At the moment, it was his expression as he stood leaning a hip against the porch rail, his ankles crossed. There was the look of a little boy at Disneyland in his eyes. He was so engrossed in the moment he hadn't bothered to mask his excitement. His face was alive with wonder and awe and, yes, respect for the drama and beauty and the power of nature and all its glory.

''Exactly,'' she said softly.

His gaze dropped to hers, puzzled. ''Exactly? Exactly *what?*''

''The look on your face. The feeling you just experienced, that's exactly why a woman like me skulks around forests and jungles and snake-infested rivers. It gets in your blood, burrows deep. Becomes more of a passion than a profession.''

He nodded thoughtfully. "Yeah. Okay. I can see where it could happen—if you were the kind of person who could get past certain basics, like air-conditioning, electricity...CNN."

His grin was back. So was his flip sophistication. But for a moment, the wonder of it all had gotten to him. He'd understood her passion. And the fact that he had didn't make his presence any easier to bear. It just made him more human, more real and far too appealing.

"I'll make tea and round up some breakfast," she said, ascending the steps and walking past Web. "Then we need to get shaking."

She was shaking just fine, Web thought as he turned and watched her walk up the steps ahead of him. Lord she had a sweet little behind.

He sighed deeply, needing to get back on level footing. Gone was the pretty pink, blond bombshell from last night. Survivalist Sadie was back, turned out in all her camouflage glory.

She wore long cargo pants today and a hooded green sweatshirt to ward off the morning chill. And of course, her boots. Steel toes if he didn't miss his guess.

"Yeah, well, your daughter wears combat boots, Mrs. Griffin," he muttered with a grim twist on the clichéd childhood taunt.

But I know your secret, little miss Salad Suit, all decked out in leafy green, he thought smugly. You've got a soft spot. A soft feminine spot—no doubt *lots* of soft feminine spots, but it was best not to venture into that dangerous territory.

Yeah. She had a weakness, all right. Satin and lace lingerie. *Pink* satin and lace lingerie. And since the wispy undies that had been hanging over the curtain rod last night were missing this morning, he had a pretty good idea she was wearing those sexy panties and bra today. And those sexy panties and bra were covering some very soft, very warm female places. Great. He was back on dangerous ground again.

It was the contrasts, he decided, that were so erotic and getting him sidetracked from his mission. Something about them was exceedingly seductive. And something about the way his brain was processing and assimilating his observations since being here was exceedingly skewed. Maybe that tree *had* hit him on the head last night.

Coffee. He needed coffee to clear out the cobwebs in his mind so he could concentrate on business. Biting the bullet, he followed her into the cabin to do a little wheedling. She'd already set the old copper tea-kettle on to boil. Chamomile and mint just wasn't going to do it for him this morning.

"Can't a person go into caffeine withdrawal or something?" he mumbled rhetorically as he checked the clothes he'd hung on the rope to see if they were dry. Mercifully, they were—at least for the most part. So were his boots.

She must have decided to take pity on him because when he came out of the bathroom dressed in his own clothes, there was an old-fashioned metal coffeepot percolating on the back burner.

Web took one whiff and groaned in appreciation. "My God, I think I love you."

"Love Charlie," she suggested. "It's his stash."

"How about if I just *like* Charlie a lot, manly man that I am and all."

She turned and there was that grin again. The one she was so stingy with that deepened her dimple so adorably. It transformed her face into a sight so pretty it took him a while to realize she wasn't just smiling, she was trying to suppress a laugh.

"What?" he said, looking down at himself to see if he was zipped and tucked.

"That's quite the outfit. Do you also have a ten-gallon hat, fur chaps and knee-high snakeskin boots back home when you want to play cowboy?"

"Hey." He made a stab at sounding offended when, in fact, he felt pretty ridiculous in his spiffy fashion-conscious canvas bush pants and multipock-eted tan safari shirt with the designer label and enough Velcro and zipper closures to cause a world-wide shortage. He'd have settled for his old NYU sweatshirt and jeans but Pearl had chosen his ward-robe for the trip and he hadn't had time to repack. "I'll have you know this is what the best-dressed ur-ban set wears when they get back to nature."

"Uh-huh." She handed him a mug full of coffee.

"C. C. Bozeman would not appreciate you making fun of his wilderness wear."

"Well, I guess if it doesn't offend you to wear it, who am I to criticize?"

"And I'm too grateful for the coffee to work up much enthusiasm over the hit to my ego."

"You ought to oil those boots, by the way, if you want them to hold up."

He grinned when her gaze made another quick and obviously unimpressed sweep of his outfit. "Yeah, well, if I intended to stick around and chop down a few trees, I might do just that."

"That reminds me. How's your shoulder?"

It was sore but tolerable. "Fine. A little stiff is all. And just so you know, these clothes are my secretary's doing."

That got her eyebrow quirked.

"She's also my godmother, and she takes her responsibility of watching out for me seriously."

"Well, let's hope you aren't taking yourself too seriously in those duds."

"Not a prayer. I feel like an action-adventure character in a low-budget movie. All I need is a pith helmet, a monocle and I'm off to find a lost tribe of the Amazon."

She smiled again, although he could see it pained her. And charmed him. "Not here, you won't."

"No. Not here," he agreed, a little baffled to find himself still as intrigued with her this morning as he had been last night in spite of his best efforts to keep his head on business. "Here, I only intended to find you. To offer you a contract. Which we absolutely are not going to talk about if I know what's good for me,'' he added with a hasty *See, I know the boundaries* smile to stall the protest forming on her lips.

The coffee tasted as good as it smelled. He carried his mug to the table to enjoy while he also enjoyed watching Tonya puttering around at the sink and stove. He admitted it was chauvinistic of him, but it was a damn fine sight to see an attractive woman cooking for him—even if she had pulled her hair back into a single braid, and she was decked out in another one of what he'd begun thinking of as her Terminator outfits.

Damn, Tyler, you've changed your tune since you spotted her little more than twelve hours ago, he reminded himself.

He scratched at the stubble he hadn't bothered to shave. He'd never been good at forming first impressions. Tonya was attractive in a self-reliant, energetic, wholesome sort of way. And it was clear she had the potential to be gorgeous if the occasion called for it.

He could picture her in designer silk. Something in blue, maybe, to match her eyes—off the shoulder, body hugging. Or in her favorite, pink. Something skimpy and lacy that showed a lot of skin as well as that saucy little body she hid so well.

''Can I help with anything?'' he asked abruptly because he had to keep his mind from wandering where it had no business going.

She cast a surprised look over her shoulder. ''Sure. You can pour some juice and set the table if you'd like. Then tell me how you like your eggs.''

''However you want to fix them is fine.''

While she cooked, he hunted up plates, glasses and mismatched silverware, then arranged them on the table. He was surprised at how homey and relaxed this all felt and not nearly as foreign and uncomfortable as it should. In addition to almost suffering caffeine withdrawal, he should be experiencing a bad case of homesickness.

But he wasn't. Truth was, except for his attraction to Tonya, he actually felt pretty relaxed. He drew a deep breath and reminded himself he wasn't here to relax, much as Pearl would have preferred it otherwise. He was here to get her to accept a contract—using whatever methods necessary. Getting chummy with his target just made sense. Still, he supposed it really wouldn't hurt him to relax just a little. It might help his cause in the long run.

"Normally, I wouldn't eat this heavily for breakfast," she said bringing two plates full of eggs to the table and setting one in front of him. "But I should probably get the cold food used up in case the electricity is out for any length of time."

"And is that a possibility?" he asked digging in.

She lifted a shoulder. "All depends on how many lines are down and how much difficulty the electrical crews have finding them and getting to them. Which reminds me. We should go check out your car and see if there's anything to be done for it."

"It's totaled," he said absently and forked in a mouthful of his breakfast. "What did you do to these eggs? They're delicious."

"It's the air up here. Everything tastes good."

"Somehow I doubt that's the reason. Where'd you learn to cook?"

"The school of necessity bred by hunger…and getting used to having meager ingredients. I carry my own spices wherever I go."

"I repeat. Delicious."

And so was she, he thought, when a pretty pink blush stole across her cheeks. Who'd have thought it? She really didn't know how to handle compliments. And she appreciated getting them—which worked just fine for him. It also gave him a little pause. She looked so young at the moment—and in that moment, he had a sudden flashback that was, in turns, vivid and murky until it finally came into focus.

He sat back and stared, dumfounded, as the pieces started falling in place. "I'll be damned."

"What?" she asked, suddenly aware of his mesmerized gaze.

"I know you. My God. All this time I've been ignoring a niggling little voice that told me you looked familiar, but it's true. You used to work for me. Didn't you?" he added when she just sat there, looking shell-shocked.

The pink that had painted her cheeks drained. Without meeting his eyes, she set down her fork and rose stiffly from the table. "More coffee?"

"Several years ago, right?" he continued, absolutely certain he was on the mark as more and more jigsaw-shaped pieces winged their way in to fill in the puzzle. "At Tyler-Lanier."

She let out a deep breath and filled his cup. "Took you long enough."

There was no pleasure in her statement. In fact, there wasn't much of anything in the way of emotion.

Web's excitement, however, grew steadily over the shock and the rush of the memories as things became clearer. "Your hair was shorter then—you wore glasses—and wasn't your name Tammy, or... something?"

She smiled but there was more disgust than humor in it. "Only because that's what you called me when you couldn't remember my name."

"Christmas party," he continued, on a roll now. "Pink sweater, black skirt."

"And too much holiday cheer," she supplied just as he recalled the rest of it.

He was vaguely aware of her clearing the plates then stacking them in the sink as it all came back. He'd arrived at the annual Tyler-Lanier Christmas party late. He'd been bored and determined to dodge a certain lawyer from the legal department who'd been coming on strong for several weeks. He'd spotted Tammy—Tonya—across the roomful of people. The place was a loud, laughter-filled echo chamber full of Christmas decorations and freely flowing champagne. He'd noticed her a couple of times in the halls during the previous few months. She'd been so cute and so shy and so obviously smitten with him.

And the night of the party, well...she *was* cute, and he'd felt a little sorry for her as she'd cast hopeful glances his way. Since he'd been having a devil of a time steering clear of—hell, what was her name? Rebecca. Yeah. Rebecca from legal with the short skirts and fast hands. He'd been in as much need of saving from Rebecca as Tonya had needed saving from the champagne.

So, he'd dodged legal eagle Rebecca and her whispered suggestion to do something that sounded very illegal with his briefs by offering Tonya a ride home. Killed two birds with one stone, was the way he'd figured it. He escaped a potential sexual harassment suit, plus he saved little newbie Tonya from being taken advantage of by snaky William Wycoff, who'd been coming on to her for the better part of an hour.

She'd been so sweet. All flushed cheeks and hero worship in her eyes, but too shy, he'd figured, to make any kind of a move.

Man, had he been wrong.

The cab had pulled up in front of the address she'd given him, he'd told her good-night and the next thing he'd known, he'd had his arms full of the softest, cuddliest, most incredible-smelling female he'd ever encountered.

For months afterward—after he'd ended the kiss and forced himself to let her go with a kind and amused smile—he'd told himself the kiss had been nothing. That the momentary explosion of sensation he'd felt when her mouth had met his had been a figment of his imagination.

But the fact was, she'd poleaxed him. That achingly innocent, erotically vulnerable kiss had damn near had him dogging her into her apartment. What

could have followed would have made him happy as
hell that night but would have plagued him with regret the next morning. Her, too.

For one thing, she'd been so young. At least she'd
seemed young. For another, he would have been taking advantage of her naiveté. But the real reason had
been because that kiss had rocked him to his core.

He'd only been twenty-three. But he'd been an experienced twenty-three, and he'd known the difference between a *let's have a great night* kiss and a
let's have a wonderful life kiss. Tonya's kiss had had
wonderful life written all over it, and in that moment
when she'd been pliable and willing in his arms, he'd
entertained the notion of forever.

It had been a brief, insane moment, but it had
scared him spitless.

It scared him spitless now as he watched her move
stiffly around the sink.

"Why didn't you say something?" he asked, in all
honesty, curious now that it was out in the open.

"Oh, gosh, let me think. Why wouldn't I have
brought up one of the most embarrassing moments in
my life?"

"Embarrassing? I thought it was flattering."

"You ran for your life," she pointed out levelly
while tossing a dish towel on her shoulder. She leaned
back against the sink, facing him.

"You were…how do I say this delicately?"

"Tipsy?" she supplied.

"Well, maybe a little. I didn't want to take advantage. And you were so young."

"What I was, was stupid."

"Had good taste in men, though," he added, playing for a smile.

She pushed out an indelicate snort. "Yeah, arrogance has always been a turn-on for me."

"There you go."

Finally, he got the smile he wanted.

"So, what happened to you? I tried to look you up after the holidays to make sure you were okay and was told you were no longer on payroll."

Actually, he'd thought so much about that kiss, he'd decided there was only one way to get it and her out of his head. He'd wanted to kiss her again and hope to hell the second experience wasn't as wild as he'd built the first one up in his mind to be.

"I got riffed."

"Riffed? As in laid off?"

She nodded. "One of many casualties of a big reduction in force."

"That's right. I remember now. It was a rough year."

"And I was low man on the totem pole."

He just stared at her for a moment, still stunned that Tonya Griffin, the photographer sought after by many publications as one of the best in the business, was the same girl who'd sent him running scared all those years ago.

It was also a shocking reminder that he'd never forgotten her sweet, desperate kiss and the feelings she'd dredged up inside of him. Feelings he'd wondered about ever since. Feelings he'd given up on ever experiencing again…that sense of finding something special. Something you hadn't known you'd lost and knowing your life would never be the same again with or without it.

He'd chosen without it and had thought at the time the choice had been the right one. He'd no more been ready to settle down at twenty-three than he was now. Back then he hadn't wanted to change his ways. He had been enjoying life and women to the fullest and hadn't wanted to be tied down to one. Now it was because he hadn't found the woman he wanted to settle down with. Hadn't found the woman who made everything go as haywire inside him as sweet little Tonya, who had poured her heart into her kiss.

Plus he had nothing to offer a woman like her. Twelve years ago, if he'd been smarter, he might have. But time had made him cynical. Experience had made him hard. Any emotions he might have once wanted to pander to, were buried somewhere under the jaded opinion he had on personal relationships in general. All he had to do was look at his own family to know he wasn't cut out for longevity in that arena.

But he still needed a professional relationship with Tonya Griffin, so he wasn't about to give up on getting her to work for the magazine. Signing her remained a do-or-die mission. Without her he lost Bozeman. Without Bozeman's dollars, *Greater Outdoors* was dead in the water before the ship set sail.

She cleared her throat and he realized his silence had made her uncomfortable. His thoughts suddenly turned to things that had no business in any equation with Tonya Griffin—then or now.

"So," he said, kicking himself back to the moment, "you struck out on your own."

"Out of necessity. I couldn't get a job in New York because I didn't have enough experience. After butting up against one brick wall too many and my money running out, I went back home and licked my wounds for a while."

"And then?"

"And then I got mad. I wanted to be a photographer. So, I became one. I shot pictures at weddings, birthday parties, graduations—anything to make a buck. On the side, I wandered around the country, catching wildlife, butterflies, whatever."

She grabbed a backpack from the corner of the cabin and started stuffing things in it. "I started sending my work to various publications, made a few sales, then made a few more sales and then one day the phone rang and a small outdoor magazine in Wisconsin actually wanted me to take a series of photographs for them."

"And the rest, as they say, is history," he added with a smile even though he felt like scowling.

He felt like his pins had been knocked out from under him ever since he realized who she was.

"Okay, look. This stroll down memory lane has been too much fun for words, but this day is going to be history if we don't get moving soon," she said, zipping up the backpack. "We've got business to take care of before I can even start shooting."

She clearly wasn't any more comfortable with all the unexpected tension vibrating between them than he was. She wanted distance from the intimacy of the cabin.

He needed some distance, too.

From the memories. From the sudden realization that all those years ago, he'd made a promise to himself that he was going to have that second kiss from her so he could put the memory of the first one to bed.

Which brought up another area of discomfort.

He could fight it and he could deny it until the bears came home, but the honest truth was a *bed* was exactly where he wanted her.

He swiped a hand over his jaw. Swore under his breath and followed her out the door. It was going to be a long few days.

A mosquito nailed him on the neck the moment he stepped outside. A helluva long few days in more ways than one.

Six

The first order of business was checking out his rental car. Tonya sighted a spot of silver sticking out of the mud about ten yards from the wrecked vehicle. She walked over and dug it out.

"Well," Web said when she handed it to him, "at least now I know what happened to my cell phone." He tried to turn it on, but even the most advanced technology couldn't withstand that much water and muck and still function.

On a heavy breath, he tossed the useless phone through the broken windshield of the rental. It hit a branch and bounced onto the soaked and glass-covered front seat.

"This car is totaled," Tonya said, standing with her hands on her hips.

"I may have mentioned that."

"And the road…" she said, ignoring him and shaking her head, "it'll be days before anyone can get back here."

"I may have mentioned that, too."

Yes, he had. And she'd been afraid he was right. Seeing it for herself made it real where, before, she had held out a small pocket of hope he may have been exaggerating. Unfortunately, he hadn't been.

He was stuck here for the foreseeable future. Which meant she was stuck with him.

It might have been tolerable before. Before, he hadn't remembered who she was, or that she'd made a total fool of herself over him.

But he had remembered and for some reason, it made the fact that he'd seen her pink panties all that much more unbearable.

Why that particular detail kept circling around her brain bugging the life out of her she'd never know.

Possibly, it was the intimacy of it all. He'd slept on her floor, sharing the night with her. He'd eaten her food. She'd touched his bare skin when she'd examined his bruise and stripped him out of his shirt and—man, oh, man, she did *not* need to think about that now. About how smooth his skin had been and how hard the muscles were beneath it. About how he'd smelled, wet with rain and running on adrenaline. And she didn't need to think about the memory of that kiss in the cab all those years ago, because it still made her light-headed and heated her blood as if it were yesterday.

Old feelings and new blended together into a thick juicy stew that kept her right at the simmering point. And *that,* she definitely didn't need.

He was still Web Tyler; she was still Tonya Griffin. And they were still two worlds apart—with the exception of whatever cosmic blip had landed them together at this place and time.

"Well," she said, determined to tough it out. He would be gone soon, she reminded herself. The road wouldn't be closed forever. "Is there anything you want to dig out of there and take back to the cabin?"

He shook his head. "With the exception of the phone, everything I brought with me was in the duffel and my carry-on."

"Then let's head down to the lake and see how Charlie's boat fared before I start shooting. The wind was from the east and would have rocked the bay pretty good. I want to make sure she survived okay."

"You're the boss," he said and fell into step behind her. "Lead on and I'll follow."

It was the follow part that bothered her. She'd never been conscious of the way she looked before. At least she hadn't been for several years. She worked hard, she dressed for it. But now it bothered her much more than it should have that the only memories Web would take with him when he left were of her as a starry-eyed nineteen-year-old and as a khaki queen with bruises on her legs and mud on her face. And of the rear view of her least favorite feature smack dab in front of his nose.

* * *

If he had to pick, Web figured Tonya's cute little tush just may be her best feature—and his eventual undoing. He'd been fantasizing about filling his palms with those sweet curvy cheeks since he'd first seen them covered in her baggy camouflage shorts.

Not that she didn't have other great features. Her hair for one thing. Something about the braid was even sexy today but he definitely preferred it the way it had looked last night. A little wet, a lot wild and as silky as any designer scarf he'd ever seen on Park Avenue. Then there were her eyes, as blue as a spring sky and her mouth, as lush and full as his favorite fruit. He was a sucker for plums and each time he'd looked at her mouth this morning, he thought about sucking and licking the juice from that sweet succulent fruit.

And if he didn't divert his thoughts, he was going to walk right up her back, he realized, slowing his stride.

All these trees. All this silence. All this time to do nothing but think about Tonya. Trees, silence and time—they were leading him straight to trouble.

As little as twelve hours ago, he'd been as happy as a damn clam. Well, not happy, but pleased over the prospect of having Tonya Griffin all to himself so he could take his time schmoozing her into signing with Tyler-Lanier.

Now he was going to have to work like hell to remind himself that his objective did not include seducing her.

"How much farther?" he grumbled, disgusted with

himself for letting his mind wander into the exact same territory he'd forbidden himself to enter.

She exhaled a sigh drenched with exaggerated patience. "You're never going to get tired of asking that question, are you?"

"You're sure we aren't lost?"

"I, however, am going to get darn tired of answering *that* one."

"Just tell me this, how the hell do you know where you're going? There are no street signs. No *streets*. Not so much as a bread crumb, Gretal. Just rocks and trees and—hey. Well, I'll be damned. A lake," he declared, realizing when they broke out of the thickest part of the forest and into a small clearing that opened up on a huge body of water.

"Happy now?"

"Happy is a relative term. Am I happy we aren't lost? Damn straight. Am I happy to see that boat washed up along the shore in the rocks over there? I don't think so."

"I was afraid something like this might have happened," she said on a deep breath. "The wind must have really stirred up the bay and she broke her moorings. Good thing it was blowing in, not out. Charlie loves that boat. If anything had happened to it, it would crush him."

Web squinted at the boat in question. He wasn't a sea dog but, best guess, it was about an eighteen footer. Aluminum. That was it. No windshield, no steering wheel—not even a motor. It was just a rowboat. An old rowboat at that. It was dented and dinged and paint was something it hadn't seen since it was new, which he was guessing was when Charlie was a young man.

"What, exactly, would a man find to love about that particular boat?" he asked, starting to get a little uneasy when he realized she'd peeled off her boots and socks while he was checking things out. "And you aren't really going to do what I think you're going to do, are you?"

"History," she said, rolling her pant legs up to her knees. "Charlie and that boat have a history. And history is important to a man like Charlie."

"History's good." He eyed the boat again. "The real question is do they have a future?"

"That's what I need to find out."

Next thing he knew, she was easing herself over the side of a narrow, weathered dock and into the water.

He was going to regret this, he just knew it, but a latent macho gene reared its ugly head and demanded he ask the question. "Do you need some help?"

She turned, shielded her eyes against the sun's glare and squinted up at him. "Do you swim?"

He did. Sort of. "Well enough."

She considered him, grinned and looked away. "How about I holler if I need you?"

That worked for him. It may be a warm day now that the storm front had passed through, but it was September and he figured the water this far north ran pretty darn cold this time of year.

Hands on his hips, he watched her wade along the

shoreline, knee-deep in the lake, working her way toward the boat where it had ended up about thirty yards away from the dock. He told himself he didn't have to feel guilty. This was her show and she obviously knew what she was doing.

The bow appeared to be fairly well beached in the rocks but a gentle chop had the aft end bobbing up and down with a hollow, scraping knock as it rocked against the stone-strewn shore.

"How does it look?" he yelled when she'd reached it and had made a cursory inspection.

"A little bruised but she appears solid. I'm going to have to bail water before I try to free her."

Standing here watching her wade over to the boat was one thing. The idea of her bailing water, then muscling the boat free while he stood on the dock, his biggest hardship a few mosquito bites and a sunburned nose, was more than his manly pride could handle.

On a deep breath, he bit the proverbial bullet. With a muttered oath, he shrugged off the backpack. After shucking his boots and socks, he rolled up his pant legs and stared hard at the water.

"I am not going to like this," he reminded himself then let out a loud, "Yowswer!" when his bare feet connected with the frigid lake.

He sucked in a harsh breath and prayed for numbness to set in. How in the hell did she stand it, he wondered as he shivered through several stiff, stilted steps. It was like walking through ice cubes—and over ice cubes. Sharp, slippery ice cubes. He hadn't experienced anything this cold since…hell, he'd never experienced anything this cold—although last night was a close second. It was only his pride—shattered as it was—that made him put one foot in front of the other. If she could do it without complaint, then, by God, so could he.

But damn, it was cold! He had to clench his jaw to keep from wincing and called himself ten kinds of a pansy every time he considered howling out with pain.

He didn't have to look over to where she stood to know she was trying not to laugh. If he were in her shoes he'd sure as the world be laughing at the stumbling, bumbling idiot lurching toward her.

"You okay?" she asked when he half waded, half fell against the side of the boat.

"Never better," he lied through gritted teeth. He gave her points for holding a straight face as he gripped a metal cleat and hauled himself upright and found his footing.

"Appreciate the help."

"Not a problem." He was going to go to hell for lying. "What can I do?"

"I bailed most of the water while you were on your way over, but I think she's still stuck on the rocks. Can you help me push her away from the shore?"

"Sure thing."

The good news was that he got out of the ice bath.

The bad news was that his legs felt like stumps. They didn't want to move on dry land. Of course, the soles of his feet were not quite numb enough, so he felt each rock dig into his tender flesh as he hobbled toward the bow of the boat.

"Okay, on three, lift and push," she said, gripping the starboard side of the bow.

He obediently latched on to the port side, jockeyed around for solid footing, braced himself and waited for her signal.

On three, he put his back into it and pushed for all he was worth.

It was another good news/bad news situation.

The good news: That sucker slid off the rocks as if it was gliding on well-oiled ball bearings. Unfortunately, after his less than impressive trip to the boat, his pride was bruised. Wanting to impress her, he put enough muscle behind his push to dislodge the U.S.S. *Eisenhower*. Momentum was an amazing thing—and he discovered its power in spades.

When the boat started moving, so did he. At least the top half of him did. But not his feet. They were dug in for a battle that never materialized. But the movement of the boat and the weight of his upper body didn't care about his feet's rock-solid position. The result was an instant, unplanned baptism.

Facedown, sucking water, he floundered like a beached cod in approximately eighteen inches of glacial lake. His life and a likely line from his obituary flashed before his eyes.

Multi-millionaire publishing mogul makes big splash. Drowns in a thimbleful of water while boat floats within reach.

He felt a pair of hands on his shoulders lift and flip him to his back, then brace him in a sitting position.

"You okay?"

It took a moment or two to catch his breath, a moment longer to regain the tattered remnants of his pride. A few more to meet the dancing blue eyes looking down at him with not nearly enough distress as far as he was concerned.

He wiped water from his face, considered her barely suppressed glee.

"Glad I could provide that good laugh you needed."

She covered her mouth behind a hand...no doubt to hide a peal of laughter. Or to disguise a kernel of guilt, he decided, finally figuring it out.

"It wasn't stuck, was it?" he asked as comprehension dawned.

Fighting her grin, she lifted her brows, shrugged. "I don't think so, no."

He nodded slowly. "So, this was an exercise in humility?"

"You looked like you wanted to help."

"And you felt compelled to provide an opportunity."

Again, she shrugged, mirth dancing in her eyes. "I aim to please."

"Uh-huh." He forced a tight smile. "Good one."

She smiled cautiously. "I thought so. And you're being a very good sport."

"Got an award for it in school. Now help me up."

He held up his hand. She hesitated for a moment and then he had her.

He locked on to her wrist with a death grip just as she got wise to his plan. "You're goin' down, cupcake."

Before she could wrench her hand away, he gave a hard tug. She landed on top of him with a shriek. Once she was down, he flipped her to her back so she was the one with her tidy little butt hugging the lake bed.

Just as she screamed, "Don't you dare!" he planted the flat of his hand on her forehead and gave her the dunking she deserved.

Tonya was laughing and choking and spitting water when she finally managed to sit up.

She shoved the hair out of her eyes and wiped the water off her face. Beside her, looking cold but smug, Web Tyler grinned in triumph.

"Okay," she conceded. "I deserved that."

"Damn straight, you did."

She wasn't sure why she'd done it. Well, okay, she knew why. Her pride had been moaning and groaning "no fair" ever since he'd dredged up that memory of her throwing herself at him back in New York twelve years ago. And her pride wanted a little justifiable retribution. So when he'd waded over to her, she'd decided now was as good a time as any to exact that revenge.

It should have been enough that he'd had to endure

the ice-cold water and the difficult and painful walk across the rocks. Somehow, however, it wasn't.

"Consider yourself an official northlander now," she said, improvising an excuse for her action as she watched him struggle to stand up.

Water dripping from him in buckets, he held out a hand to help her up. "Oh, so that was an *initiation*," he concluded with enough sarcasm to make sure she understood he didn't believe her for a minute. "That's how you plan to justify the case of pneumonia I'm going to have when I finally leave here?"

She took his hand, started to rise then found herself flat on her butt in the water again when he abruptly let go.

"Whoops. Sorry. My hand must have slipped...or something." He neither sounded nor looked apologetic. "Wanna try for two in a row?"

She could see she'd surprised him when he offered his hand again and she took it. At the same time, she hooked her foot around the back of his knee and gave a hard tug.

When the splashing stopped, he was facedown in the drink again but managed to flip over by himself this time.

They glared at each other, sitting waist-deep in water.

"Nice belly flop," she said brightly. "You looked like Hulk Hogan flying off the ropes in a WWF meet."

"This is really fun." He raked his hair back from his face and she couldn't help but notice how the water clung to his thick lashes. "But if you do that one more time—"

"You'll what? Leave me here all by myself to find my way back to the cabin?"

Her threat rang as clear as the glacial lake water, which had plastered his shirt to his chest like wallpaper. Which meant her shirt was plastered to her breasts the same way.

"Oh. I see." He narrowed his eyes and nodded. "You just have to play dirty, don't you?"

"Let's just say I know when to press my advantage."

She started to rise, but he snagged her arm and pulled her back down beside him. "You aren't the only one with an advantage here, cupcake."

His voice had dropped. So had his gaze. She looked down at herself. Her wet shirt left nothing to the imagination—including the very hard tips of her nipples. As cold as she was, she knew the icicle factor wasn't totally responsible for her body's reaction; the Web Tyler factor had a finger in that pie, too.

She swallowed and forced herself to meet his eyes again—just before he pulled her flush against him and kissed her.

Mistake, mistake, mistake!

The warning rattled around in Web's head like a pinball banging against the bumpers, but at the moment he didn't care. He was so angry with her, so exhilarated, so cold and so damn turned on he didn't give two hoots about mistakes or consequences or even the rock that was going to make a bruise the size of Times Square on his hip. He simply picked the option that felt the best and went with it.

She felt good. Her body was wet and lush where her hip met his, and her breasts with their diamond-hard little peaks pressed against his chest like drill bits.

Her lips were ice cold and tight with protest and surprise at first, but when he cupped her jaw and encouraged her to open up for his tongue, inside her mouth he encountered all sleek, wet heat.

And that's when he stopped thinking altogether, stopped shivering and simply experienced.

On a groan of pure pleasure, he lifted her up, set her on his lap and suddenly oblivious to the icy water, he plummeted into the kiss like a cliff diver plunging from a thirty-foot drop. It was all wild, out-of-control free fall. And he sank into it like a stone. Ate it up like ice cream—savoring every second, paying great attention to the explosion of flavors and textures and sensations.

Indulgence, that's all he had on his mind now. There was no thought of retribution when he tunneled his fingers up and under her wet braid to cup her head in his hand and realign their mouths for a better fit. No thought of paybacks in the vicinity when he settled her against a monster erection that lay to rest any speculation about cold water and shrinkage.

And when she did a little moaning of her own and opened her mouth wider, initiating a seek-and-destroy-his-control mission with her tongue, the satisfaction he felt had nothing to do with getting even and everything to do with mutual need.

Sweet. He'd known she would be sweet. He'd remembered—all these years he'd remembered the unstructured exuberance of her kiss in the back of that cab. Had been running from the irrational need and the unrelenting want to experience her again ever since.

Her passion was everything he remembered—and yet more than he'd expected or hoped for. She was both untutored but intuitive as they took the kiss to a deeper level that was either going to end with them both naked and extremely happy or drowned.

Someone had to start thinking here. Looked like it was going to be him because her arms were wrapped around his neck now, and she was making soft little erotic sounds of need.

Heart pounding, he lifted his head with a groan then kissed her quick when she followed his mouth with hers. He caressed her slim throat with splayed fingers and pressed his forehead to hers. "What do you say we take this back to the cabin?"

She drew a quivering breath. Looked up at him through spiky, wet lashes. And abruptly jumped off his lap.

"What the hell was that?" she demanded, splashing water and looking horrified. She swiped a hand wildly over her hair and to his eternal disappointment tugged her shirt away from her breasts.

"I believe it's commonly referred to as kissing?"

He forced himself to stand, too puzzled over her sudden outrage to do much more than stare at her.

When her eyes narrowed in accusatory anger, his own anger reached flash point. "Hey…from my perspective, you appeared to be a fairly willing participant."

"I'm rowing the boat back to the dock," she snapped and waded over to the bobbing craft.

Hands on his hips, he watched her hike herself up and over the side, position the oars and start rowing.

"Oh, don't worry about me," he grumbled as she rowed so hard she left a wake. "I'm good here. I'll just walk back. Not a problem."

What the hell had gotten into her? he wondered. She had been participating…and at a level several notches up from "fairly willing." She'd been all over him.

And now he was mad as hell, too. So mad, he barely felt the sharp jab of the rocks as he stumbled back toward the dock.

Mad at himself for having the brain freeze that had triggered that kiss. Mad at her for being mad at him. Mad at fate for landing him in the same lake with a woman who should have stayed in his past and who obviously would have preferred the same of him.

This was Pearl's fault. First thing when he got back to New York, he was going to take away her key to the executive washroom. That'd fix her meddling wagon for landing him in this predicament.

Just like little Miss Runaway Rosie, who was already at the dock, tying up the boat, had fixed him just now.

Fixed him good.

He didn't want to like Tonya. He didn't want to admire her spunk. Or to admit that it was the emotional tug he'd felt toward her all those years ago that had him dodging serious relationships ever since.

And he sure as the world didn't want to take her to bed.

Like hell he didn't.

His unshaved skin felt like sandpaper against his palm as he scrubbed it across his jaw and settled himself down. He wanted her. But he wanted the signed contract more. At least he told himself he did, and that's what was going to see him through this.

No more playing kissie face with Tonya Griffin.

No more fantasizing about making love with her on that big old squeaky bed.

No more mistakes. Period.

Seven

It was a long, silent walk back to the cabin. Tonya would never admit it, at least not to Web, but the trembling she experienced had as much to do with her reaction to his kiss as it did with her cold, wet clothes. Not to mention her anger at herself for being so stupid.

He'd kissed her. Damn him.

And she'd kissed him back. Damn her.

And damn her heart that slammed into irregular beats every time she thought about it.

Potent. That word came to mind again. Him and his incredible, wonderful mouth. Him and his busy tongue. Him and his roaming hands that had made her hot and achy and prompted her to wrap her arms around his neck and latch on as if he was a life preserver and she'd been drowning in a sea of need.

The only thing she needed was to get away from him before she was the one suggesting they pick up where they left off.

"I changed my mind," she said abruptly when they reached the cabin. "I'm going on my shoot alone."

"Fine."

He looked away and she couldn't tell if he was glowering or grinning.

Whatever. That was his problem. *He* was her problem, though, and she needed some distance and some time to get a grip on how she was going to handle him.

After a quick change into dry clothes, she loaded her camera, shouldered the backpacks he'd set by the door and stomped off into the woods. It was all so ridiculous, she thought, climbing over a downed tree. She had no one but herself to blame. She'd baited him, humiliated him and then cried foul when he'd launched a retaliatory strike.

"You got exactly what you deserved," she muttered, then made herself slow down. She was making so much noise she'd never find a subject. What she'd gotten was more than she could handle and now she was going to have to live with it.

She was going to have to live with the memory of that incredible kiss and his suggestion to go back to the cabin to finish what they'd started.

And, she realized as she hiked deeper into the forest, she was going to face him again at the end of the day…knowing full well that she really wanted to finish it, too.

* * *

Time, distance and space had done the trick. It was all she'd ever needed to turn a muddy stream of thought into a sparkling clear brook, Tonya assured herself as she made her way back to the cabin several hours later. She didn't think well when she was crowded…and Web had crowded her for almost twenty-four hours now. At least he'd crowded her mind.

Her solitary foray into the woods had helped. She hadn't shot any film, but she'd put everything back in perspective now.

That…*incident* in the water with Web had been no big deal. Just a heat-of-the-moment episode sparked by adrenaline.

He probably felt as much regret about it as she did. So, she'd be big about it, she decided as she entered the clearing and the cabin came into view. She'd apologize for suckering him in and setting him up. And she'd suggest they simply forget about the…*incident.*

It was easier to think about it that way. It was a nebulous term rather than specific and that lessened its importance. If she thought in specifics…like the feel of his hot, hungry mouth covering hers, like the way the strong column of his neck had felt beneath her hands, like the thickness of his erection pressing against her hip—

She groaned. If only she could *stop* thinking in specifics.

What was wrong with her? She should have worked that kiss out of her system by now.

"Like you worked the one twelve years ago out of your system?" she muttered aloud.

She was hopeless.

And he was—what was he, exactly? Out of reach? Out of bounds? Out of her league?

Yeah. All that and more.

Hadn't she learned her lesson? Men like Web Tyler didn't take women like her seriously. Men didn't take her seriously, period. At least not the ones she'd become involved with after she'd left New York. One or two, she'd actually thought she might be able to make a life with, until she'd realized that their idea of compromise was for her to give up her dreams for theirs. It had hurt that they hadn't seen her as an equal or that they hadn't seen her work as serious. Hurt so much it just became easier to bury herself deeper in her photography because she avoided painful emotional entanglements that way.

Like the one brewing with Web.

And it was brewing, whether she wanted it to or not.

Speaking of brewing, she stopped a few feet from the cabin steps. She inhaled deeply and smelled...food?

She squinted toward the open windows. The September breeze rustled the curtains. A light shone over the sink.

Light?

Well, at least something good had happened. If the electricity was back on then the road would most likely be cleared soon, too. And then he could go about his merry way and let her get back to what she did best. Work. Alone. Without the kind of distractions he brought with him. That's what she wanted, right?

Right, she assured herself and ignored the niggling little feeling of loss already crowding out the full feeling in her chest.

Bracing for what could be an uncomfortable confrontation, she stared at the steps. Then, on a deep breath, she climbed them and reached for the door.

Web watched as Tonya emerged from the woods looking a bit like a wood nymph in combat boots. When he caught himself smiling, he quickly dropped the curtain and made himself ignore the little lurch of pleasure he felt just watching her. Those kinds of thoughts were going to lead straight to defeat in more ways than one. He wasn't going there again. That kiss had been a mistake. He knew it. She knew it. End of story. Tonya Griffin was off-limits for anything other than business.

That's what had gotten him through the afternoon. Business. He needed the contract, not a fast tumble— even though he had no doubt it would be unbelievably satisfying. So he'd kept his hands busy and his mind occupied.

All and all, he'd been a very busy boy. And he was pretty darn pleased with himself, even though it was stupid to get so pumped up over his little achievements. He'd done nothing but bumble around ever since he'd arrived from the city, so accomplishing

something constructive on her turf felt damn good—
even if it was small potatoes.

He had all kinds of surprises ready for Ms. Griffin.
Not, he assured himself, because he wanted to please
her. Oh, no. What he wanted was to astound her—
and to reestablish his image as competent, command-
ing and in control.

Moving fast, he plopped himself down at the table
with one of the old Louis L'Amour books he'd found
on the bookshelf. He was slouched in a chair, one
ankle crossed over a knee and, by all appearances,
engrossed in the book when in fact he hadn't read
word one, when the door swung open.

"You're back," he said brightly, the picture of
cool, unperturbed nonchalance as he looked up.

Standing in the open doorway, she scowled from
him to the book then finally shut the door behind her.
She dropped her gear on the floor by her feet.

"What's this?" Suspicion narrowed her eyes as she
took in the table.

He'd set it for two, complete with a candle and a
bouquet of fresh wildflowers he'd found growing at
the edge of the encampment.

"Let's call it an apology for what happened this
morning." He smiled with just the right amount of
hesitance.

He could tell by the look on her face that she
wasn't sure she was buying it. She would, though,
when she discovered his other surprises, so he left it
at that.

"When did the electricity come on?"

"Oh, that. Far as I know it's still off." He feigned renewed interest in the book and said, oh so offhandedly, "I found a generator in the shed and started it up."

He'd been waiting all afternoon to deliver that line. Just toss it out there like a discard during a game of gin, as if it was no big deal. As if it hadn't taken him the better part of three hours to get that sucker up and running and he hadn't mauled the heck out of his fingers in the process.

"Generator? There's a generator?"

"In the shed. Behind the woodpile." He loved the surprise in her voice. She hadn't moved from the door. It said a lot about her comfort level. She didn't know what to make of this new competent Web and the idea that he knew something she didn't.

"You knew how to start the generator?"

He hadn't, but he did now and he hoped to hell he never had to tackle anything that complicated and cantankerous again.

"Well...sure." He glanced at her, his shrug saying, *I own the Y chromosome, after all. Why wouldn't I?*

Frowning, she slipped off her hiking boots then lifted her backpack onto the table. "What were you doing in the shed?"

"The wood supply in the cabin was low. I was hunting for an ax. I split some logs while I was at it." *Manly man that I am.*

Her head swiveled to the woodstove. He hid a grin when she blinked at the nice tidy stack of firewood he'd carted in.

"Oh, and I put out food for when the bears start wandering in. Was that okay?"

Her hand stalled as she drew a water bottle from her bag. "You fed the bears?"

Again, he shrugged, still feigning interest in the book. "Figured you'd be tired. What with all that hiking. And rowing," he added, finally looking up and giving her a speculative grin.

She blinked at him, clearly confused by all this benevolence. Which was exactly what he'd been playing for. For the first time since he'd arrived, he had the upper hand. Now the kicker.

"Oh, and I made dinner. Some fish in the freezer had started to thaw before I found the generator. Walleye, if the package was marked right. Hope it's good baked."

"Baked," she repeated, barely able to keep her jaw from dropping.

"With a little parsley and lemon butter. And I experimented with some of your spices. Think that'll work?"

"Um, yeah. It'll work just…just fine. I…I think I'll take a quick shower."

She blinked at him again, opened her mouth as if she was going to say something, thought better of it and walked directly to the bathroom, the scent of her mosquito spray trailing in her wake.

He'd have done a little victory lap around the cabin if he hadn't thought it would rattle the windows and send her scurrying back out to see what was wrong.

He was liking this. A lot. He liked being back in

control—although control was another one of those relative terms.

He also liked having her off guard. He'd counted on surprise to accomplish that and, so far, it had worked like a charm.

And now *he'd* do the charming—strictly business charming—and introduce the idea of the contract again. Over fish that she hadn't had to prepare and, if he did say so himself, smelled mighty fine.

Oh, yeah. He was back in control now. No more straying into dangerous territory. No more kissing. No more thinking about kissing. No more thinking about that soft, lush body, that golden tangle of hair, that mouth that was made for kissing.

He stopped himself abruptly. Drew a deep breath. No more. Period. The stakes were too high to screw this up.

He was screwed, Web thought fifteen minutes later when Tonya opened the bathroom door.

Oh, man. The floral and melon scents wafting out of the room were so essentially female, so intrinsically seductive, he felt the first slow slip and slide of his control.

When she emerged from the tiny room, her golden hair wet and flowing, her unassumingly pretty face with its soft summer tan scrubbed clean and glowing, he felt a little piece of earth give way beneath his feet.

She'd traded her camouflage for jeans. Old jeans

faded to almost white and tight. So tight they hugged every adorable curve.

Her sweater was red. Something lightweight with a turtleneck. And it was snug. Not quite as snug as her jeans but snug enough to showcase those incredible breasts she usually worked so hard to hide.

He knew what they felt like pressed against him now. He knew the soft, yielding fullness of them, knew the shape of her nipples when they were puckered tight with cold, wanted to know the shape and the feel of them when they were puckered tight with desire.

He was *sooo* screwed.

Seeing her like this, all he could think about was that if he went into the bathroom, he'd probably find those pink panties and bra washed and hanging over the shower rod. Which made him wonder about what she was wearing next to her skin now. Would it be lace or satin? Bikini or thong? Red, like her sweater? Pink like her lips? Black, like his mood?

Royally screwed.

Everything about her looked so soft and approachable—and uncertain, right down to her pretty pink bare feet.

Contract, he thought. Command and control. Business. Important business.

"Feel better?" he asked digging deep for a courteous distance.

"Much."

She hunted around in a bureau and came up with a brush that she proceeded to work through her hair.

The process mesmerized him. The glide of the brush through all that long, damp hair. The thrust of her breasts against her sweater as she raised her arms. The graceful arch of her back and the curve of her bottom when she leaned forward, flipping her hair down toward the floor as she worked the brush through the underside.

What? What was with him? He'd been with plenty of women. Women who, unlike Tonya, worked at being alluring and sophisticated. Women who knew the score. Women who wouldn't be hurt at the end of a brief affair. Which he was *not* going to have with her.

''I think the fish is done,'' he said, telling himself not to panic. He was simply going to follow his plan and do nothing more than charm her into signing that stupid contract.

''I found some greens so I tossed a salad, too. And stuck some potatoes in the oven to bake.''

She straightened and all that glorious hair fell like a cascading curtain down her back. Gaze fastened on him, she narrowed her eyes and for the first time since she'd arrived back at the cabin she made no effort to mask her reaction.

''What's this about, Tyler?''

He set the salad on the table. ''What's what about?''

She swept a hand around the cabin. ''All of this. Chopping and carting wood. Feeding the bears. Making dinner. None of it seems like your bailiwick to me.''

She was so right. Except for the dinner part, it was

all as foreign to him as the feelings he kept fighting for her. He shoved his hand into a scorched and stained oven mitt and retrieved the fish and the potatoes from the oven.

"Bailiwick. Now there's a word I haven't heard in a while."

She blinked at him, crossed her arms beneath her breasts. Where his gaze followed like a laser beam locked on target.

On a deep breath, he averted his gaze to her face. Smiled. "Granted, all this deep-woods stuff is not my thing, but, for your information, I'm a darn fine cook. It started out as research for a cooking magazine we published several years ago and became a hobby."

"Okay. I'll give you that—"

"I hear a *but* in there." He set the fish in the middle of the table and pulled out a chair for her, inviting her to sit down. Wishing it could be on his lap. "But, why bother with the other?"

Her silence said he'd nailed it in one.

He shrugged and sat, filling her plate then his as he talked. "This may come as a surprise, but I'm not used to feeling inadequate. It tends to make me cranky—like I was this morning when I dunked you. This is my way of soothing my dinged pride and apologizing for dunking you. I was out of line."

"Well—" she sat hesitantly then scooted her chair up to the table "—since you're being so charitable, I apologize, too. For setting you up. It was a little mean-spirited."

She looked down at the hands she'd clasped on her

lap. Gave a one-shouldered shrug. "My pride was a little bruised, too."

Okay. This was the part where he should smile generously, put on his conciliatory face and change the subject to something like, oh, say, the contract. But his heart had started hammering the moment she'd sat down within touching and smelling distance. His palms had started itching to get his fingers in that damp, silky hair. And the next thing he knew, with no prompting from his brain, he was asking the last thing in the world he needed to ask.

"Should I apologize for kissing you, too?"

Her head came up. She looked as tense as he felt. And if he wasn't mistaken, she was also as aroused by the memory of that kiss as he was. She swallowed, licked her lips, then lowered her head to her plate. "The fish looks delicious."

He stared at the top of her head for a moment, knowing she was right. That kiss was no place they needed to go.

And yet, he felt an unsettling sense of loss when he picked up his fork and followed her lead. "Bon appétit."

The next morning Tonya rose, as usual, at daylight. That was over three hours ago. She'd fed the bears then spent the time since developing film in the make-shift darkroom she'd set up in Charlie's garage...and thinking about last night.

Web had been the perfect gentleman. He'd even done the dishes after dinner which had *really* amazed her. He'd also been cordial and funny and gracious when she'd beat him again at gin.

And he hadn't flirted with her. Not once. He'd said good-night, crawled into his sleeping bag and that's the last she'd heard from him.

Which was good, she assured herself with a scowl and wondered why she felt so grumpy.

On a sigh, she spaced the dried prints she'd just developed on the kitchen table then carefully inspected the finished photographs in hopes they'd take her mind off thoughts she had no business thinking. Like the way it had felt when Web had kissed her in the lake. About his husky suggestion to take it back to the cabin.

Should I apologize for kissing you, too?

His question at the dinner table had haunted her all night. So had her cowardly avoidance of it.

"Get over it," she muttered and focused on the photographs again and eventually became lost in the images.

They were the shots she'd taken of Damien the other day. The day Web had arrived.

She was deep in concentration, exceedingly pleased with what she was seeing when Web walked into the cabin.

"I think we probably need to ration our time using the generator," he said, wiping his hands on a wad of paper towels. "We used about a third of the gas yesterday and it's hard telling…"

His voice trailed off as he walked up behind her. She smelled him before she sensed his heat. Soap and shaving cream and that wonderful woodsy scent that he'd brought with him from outside.

"Amazing," he uttered.

She glanced over her shoulder, saw that he was looking at her photos.

"Yeah. I agree. He is amazing, isn't he?"

"I meant the photographs. You're… What you've captured here…they're incredible."

"Damien tends to bring out the best in me."

"Damien?" He chuckled softly and the sound resonated along her skin like a soft, sensual breeze. "I don't recall any Republican politician by that name."

"Even Charlie recognized that this guy was in a class of his own." She moved to the stove to refill her mug with hot water…anything to get away from him. She reacted too strongly, felt too much when he was near. "Damien's the bear I was filming the day you showed up."

"The day I showed up? Wait. How did you get these developed? Have you been holding out on me? Did you use a digital camera and you've got a computer and printer hidden around here somewhere?"

"No, no computer. And no digital camera. I'll stick with my Nikon F1, thank you very much. I much prefer film to digital and traditional thirty-five-millimeter film is a safer bet when it gets cold than digital cards. As for developing the film, I threw together a small makeshift darkroom in Charlie's garage shortly after I arrived."

"You're a traditional kind of girl, huh?"

"Usually."

Usually, she was in total control of her actions and reactions. But since yesterday and that kiss, she was on shaky ground. She felt anything but conventional around him.

He appeared to be just fine with what had happened, apparently already forgetting it. She needed to follow his lead. Her head was on board with the plan. Now, if she could just get her libido and her heart to follow.

The thought stopped her cold.

Heart? Her heart didn't have anything to do with this. Maybe she had a little carryover crush from years ago, but that was just…

What did it mean when a woman fell for a man when she was nineteen and she still thought about him twelve years later? What did it mean when her heart still flip-flopped at the sound of his voice, at the touch of his hand, at the slightest smile?

It didn't mean love, that's for sure, she assured herself, fighting a swelling panic. It couldn't mean love.

It just couldn't. She wouldn't let it.

She glanced at him as he studied the pictures, felt herself melt merely looking at the strong lines of his profile and quickly looked away. The next words out of his mouth provided the catalyst she needed to regain her solid footing.

"These really are amazing, Tonya. Forget the salary offer I made. I'll double it if you'll sign the contract."

Eight

After his astounding second offer, it became easier, Tonya told herself, to retain that emotional and physical distance. And the next couple of days she managed to do just that. Web wasn't looking for romance. He was still wheeling and dealing and determined to sign her; that, after all, was his sole purpose for being here. And that kiss…well, it had happened in the heat of the moment. A mistake. An anomaly.

The financial security he offered was tempting, she thought as they waited in a blind made of rocks and pine boughs near the last spot she'd seen Damien, hoping he'd show up again. Yes, the salary was very tempting. But because the prospect of being around him tempted her more, she stuck to her guns.

"You don't have to sit here you know," she whispered when he fidgeted. ''I'm used to this. So are my muscles. Yours aren't.''

''Trying to get rid of me, Griffin?'' he whispered back with a grin.

Tonya had been trying to get rid of him for an hour, but the man was as stubborn as the gum Jason Kimble had stuck in her hair in the sixth grade.

The close quarters were getting to her. She couldn't move a toe without bumping his knee, couldn't lean forward without brushing his shoulder, couldn't turn her head without bumping his nose.

At least she didn't have to breathe the expensive aftershave he usually wore that smelled so male and sensual. She'd told him in no uncertain terms that, if he went with her on a shoot, he was to wear no overt scents.

''Scares away the bears,'' she'd explained, although truth be told, it had a much stronger affect on her.

''I can't imagine,'' he mused aloud now, more to himself than to her.

Sunlight filtered down between the towering pines and cast flickering shadows across his face. Her heart did a little flip and she had to draw a breath to settle herself. ''Can't imagine what?''

''Living out here. Forty years, is that what you said? Charlie has lived out here for forty years?''

''More like sixty.''

''How did he stand the solitude? The quiet? I mean, yeah, after being here a while I do see the appeal. It's beautiful. The air—it's so pure. But—'' he stopped, shook his head "—it's so remote. How could he not get lonely?"

"You need to meet him," she heard herself saying. "Then you'll understand. Charlie's very self-sufficient. Reminds me of my grandfather Bennett. Take charge, content, confident. And it's not like he's out here twenty-four/seven/three-hundred sixty-five days by himself. There are neighbors. And family. They come to see him. He goes to see them."

"But he's tied to the bears."

"He loves the bears. He doesn't consider them an obligation. He considers them family and he likes them for company. No games. No demands except the obvious."

"Food."

"And a safe haven."

She looked at the lowering sun. "Damien's not going to show. We should head back to the cabin for the day."

She was still grubbing around for her various pieces of equipment when she realized he'd stood and offered a hand.

It would have been more obvious if she'd ignored it than if she'd taken it.

"Thanks," she said, and quickly let go while the feel of his big warm hand lingered on her fingers. "I can take that," she said when he reached for her heavy backpack.

"A deal's a deal." He grinned and shouldered the pack. "But I will beat you at gin one of these nights before I leave."

"Yeah, well, you'd better hurry," she said, setting out for the cabin, "because I have a feeling they'll have the road cleared within a day or two."

And none too soon, she thought to herself as they made their way through the woods. Web Tyler was just too much. Too much of a reminder of what her life was lacking. Too much man for any woman with a healthy libido to ignore. Too much for this woman to resist if he ever decided to turn up the charm.

Which he wouldn't hesitate to do if he thought it would get her to sign his precious contract.

Web sat on the top tread of the cabin steps. He cradled a mug of lukewarm coffee in his hands and watched the sunset sky. In September, in Northern Minnesota, the days were short and the nights came early and rapidly grew cool. In the past fifteen or so minutes the changing palette of colors to the west had shifted from brilliant apricot and red-gold to luminous lavender and pearly gray. When the door opened behind him and Tonya stepped outside, dusk was almost history and night was setting in without attitude. Just a slow gentle glide toward darkness.

The first glimmer of the North Star appeared low, just above the tree line. An eggshell moon, on the waning side of half, drifted in and out of wispy, ghost-gray clouds and bathed the coming night in a filtered, dreamy glow.

"It's been so long since I've seen anything but a city sky at night. I'd forgotten how beautiful it can be," he said, aware of her standing behind him.

He looked up and over his shoulder to see her cross her arms under her breasts and lift her face to the sky. "It's definitely one of the perks of my job."

"I recognize the crickets, but what else am I hearing?"

She listened for a moment. "Night songs," she finally said softly. "Just night songs."

"Night songs. I like that."

He stood then, set his mug on the porch railing. She looked so young standing beside him. And so beautiful. He'd given up his flirting game a couple of days ago because he'd realized it would lead him straight into trouble. So he'd worked hard to keep a professional distance. So had she. And the fact that they'd both had to work to keep that distance wasn't lost on him. Or on her.

He saw her shiver, recognized it wasn't only from the chill. Sexual tension had a life of its own. Signs of its own. Unmistakable signs and there'd been plenty over the past few days. The subtle shift of a gaze to avoid the intense heat. The reflexive flinch to avoid a touch. A laugh that came a little too quick, a little too forced to cover the yearning that lay just beneath the surface but never fully retreated.

They'd both been playing the avoidance game. Too long.

He was tired of fighting his basic instincts. He was tired of avoiding her. Tired of dancing around what he really wanted. He had another kind of dance in mind tonight.

Acting on pure impulse, he took her hand, ignored

her startled look and dragged her down the steps with him.

"Since the night is making such beautiful music, it would be a shame for us to waste it." When they reached the ground, he turned her to face him. "Dance with me."

It was on the tip of her tongue to tell him no. He could see it in her eyes. But he could also see the longing and that's the answer he chose to accept.

Before she could gather her wits about her, he pulled her into his arms, started moving to a slow, swaying rhythm he heard in his head. She must have heard it, too, because when she decided to give in to the moment and the music, she followed his lead and moved with him as if they'd been practicing these steps for years.

Several moments passed where they just swayed together, getting used to the feel of each other, the scents, the electric charge constantly pulling at them.

"What are we doing?" she asked carefully.

"Just dancing, cupcake. Just dancing. Let's just leave it at that. For now."

Around them, night closed in like a blanket. He pulled her a little tighter in his arms.

"Why is it," he murmured as he lifted both of her hands to drape them around his neck, "that I've lived my entire life acting on knowledge-based, calculated actions and I'm here for three days and suddenly I'm relying on impulse to lead the way?"

He wrapped his arms around her waist, pulled her

closer, pressing his palms at the small of her back, spreading his fingers wide over her slim hips.

"Maybe it's the fresh air?" she suggested in a small voice.

He chuckled and turned his cheek to lie against the silk of her hair. "I suppose that's a possibility."

A slim one. It was so strange. Since he'd stumbled on to Tonya, he felt more spontaneous and alive than he had in longer than he could remember. He wasn't moving and shaking things up on Sixth Avenue where money and power had always been both his driving force and his reward, but he felt more vital, more essential than he had in ages. And he seriously doubted it had anything to do with the fresh air.

"I think it might have more to do with something else."

"Oh?"

She was so much more than he'd expected. She was funny and bright and even though she constantly tried to hide it, she was beautiful inside and out. He'd been doing his damnedest to see her as nothing but a Pollyanna pixie in olive drab. In truth, however, it had become increasingly obvious that he wasn't just attracted to Tonya, who, beneath all her staunch individualism and Wilderness Wanda clothes, was fun-loving and heartbreakingly naive, he liked her. A lot.

Besides being gorgeous and sexy, she was intelligent and sweet and so sincere that he couldn't help but be touched by her. And she had no idea how attractive she truly was. She was also an incredibly gifted photographer. Her pictures of the bears were exciting, poignant and sobering and showed even greater insight into her soul.

All that together still didn't cover what he'd started to suspect he felt for her.

But he didn't want to go there right now. He didn't want to analyze or overthink or ruin the moment by muddying things up with thoughts he hadn't fully processed.

Her skin glowed dewy gold in the moonlight. He lifted a hand to her jaw, tipped her face to his. And gave up the fight. "You know I'm going to kiss you, don't you? You know I need to kiss you."

His heart pumped in double time, slamming inside his chest when she tipped her head back and met his gaze.

Desire. It drifted in her eyes like smoke. Heated his blood like a bonfire.

And he was a goner.

It was like a dam had burst inside him and a flood of testosterone so intense and so reckless rolled right over any common sense he'd ever owned, squelching it flat in the wake of a tidal wave of want.

With no thought of slowing down, much less stopping, he dragged her into a deep, carnal kiss.

"If you don't want this, tell me to stop," he whispered against her lips even as he seduced her with his mouth and his hands. "Tell me now."

"Stop," she murmured obediently wrapping her arms around his neck and hooking a leg around his thigh.

He groaned, buried his hand in her hair and luxuriated in the feel of all that golden silk. With a gentle tug, he loosened the tie on her braid, finger combed her hair until it was heavy and loose and slid through his fingers like water. When she whimpered and moved closer, he ran his hands down her sweet behind until he reached the back of her thighs and lifted her, wrapping her legs around his waist.

"You really want me to stop?" he whispered as he trailed hungry, biting kisses down her throat, back to her jaw and finally covered her mouth again.

"No." The word drifted out on a quivering sigh as he walked them toward the cabin, up the steps and inside. Kissing and caressing until they were both squirming to get closer, he kicked the door closed behind them and walked her toward the bed.

"You're sure?"

"I'm sure I want you to stop talking." She made a hungry, throaty sound against his neck and, knotting her hands in his hair, pulled his mouth down to hers. "Just stop talking."

She didn't have to tell him twice. Her hands were doing all the talking for her now, anyway. And her body. And her incredible, edible mouth.

When his knees hit the bed he toppled with her, bracing his weight above her on his arms so he didn't crush her beneath him. The old mattress sagged; the springs complained of their joined weight as he pressed her against the quilt with his body, making a place for himself between her thighs.

"This is crazy," he murmured against the silk of

her hair as he buried his face in that lovely curve
where neck met shoulder.

"You're talking again." Her hands moved frantically, grabbing handfuls of his shirt and tugging it out
of his waistband. "I can think of much better things
for you to do with your mouth."

With a groan, he rolled to his back, taking her with
him, then helped her with the buttons.

"Now you," he said as he hiked himself up enough
to shrug out of his shirt.

She was an amazing sight, straddling his lap, her
hair wild around her face, her cheeks flushed, her lips
swollen from his kisses.

Without hesitation, she crossed her arms in front of
her, latched on to the hem of her sweater and tugged
it up and over her head.

A spear of heat arrowed straight to his groin as he
sat there, his stiff arms holding him upright, his hands
planted behind him in the mattress.

Ever since he'd seen her underwear drying in the
bathroom he'd been wondering what color she was
wearing against her skin. Now he knew.

It wasn't pink tonight. Or white. Her bra was
black—and what there was of it was lacy and sheer.
Very sheer. Her nipples were dainty and defined as
they pressed in stark relief against the gossamer fabric—about an inch away from his mouth.

"Sweet Tonya," he whispered and unable to wait
a moment longer, dipped his head that infinitesimal
distance and took her in his mouth.

She made a thready sound of need and leaned into

him, offering her breast with uninhibited abandon. He
opened his mouth wide, scraped sheer fabric and
warm, soft woman with his teeth before drawing her
nipple into his mouth and sucking her through black
lace.

He heard her breath catch on a little sigh as he
pulled slowly away, sucking as he went, drawing her
with him before letting go. With a gentle nudge of
his nose, he encouraged her to offer her other breast.

She did, rising slightly to her knees and pressing
forward so he could take her fully in his mouth. She
liked it. He could tell. He loved it. All that heat. All
that pillowy softness confined in lace. All that
woman.

She cried out when he gently bit her then reached
behind her back. When the clasp gave, he latched on
to the cup with his teeth and dragged it out of his
way. He wanted his tongue on her bare nipple. He
wanted flesh against flesh, willing and wet, generous
and warm.

He lurched forward, sitting up straighter and
pressed his palms between her shoulder blades to
draw her closer. Her hair fell across his face, feath-
ered across the back of his fingers like spun gold. The
skin beneath his palms felt as smooth as velvet, an
erotic contrast to the hands gripping his shoulders in
both desperation and demand.

Her desperation fired his blood to boiling and he
shifted them again until she was lying on her back
and he was kneeling above her, straddling her hips,
taking in the sight of her. Her hair spilled across the

calico quilt, her lush breasts were shiny and wet from
his mouth—and her small, greedy hands were reaching for his belt buckle.

When had she become so beautiful? When had she
transformed into this wanton, sexual creature who
tempted like the original sin? And when had he gone
out of his mind with wanting her?

He didn't know. Didn't care as her slender fingers
managed to unsnap the button at his waist then slowly
worked down the zipper.

He groaned when she reached inside and touched
him through his shorts, stilled her when her hot little
hands cupped him.

"You don't know," he whispered, leaning down
and kissing her long and deep, "how much it pains
me to do this, but I've got to go get something," he
said on a groan before rising from the bed and going
in search of his shaving kit.

He may not have been a Boy Scout, but he always
believed in being prepared and in this moment he
thanked the gods of safe sex that he never left home
without protection.

When he returned to the bed, she'd undone the snap
at her waist and was reaching for her own zipper.

"Oh, no." He planted a knee deep in the mattress
at her hip. "That's my job."

A small smile tilted her lips as she hesitated then
deferred to his wishes in a way that stopped his heart.
She lifted her arms and let them drop so her hands
were palms up on either side of her head just as she
tipped her hips ever so slightly off the bed.

He tossed a foil packet on the bed beside her hand, took his own sweet time drinking in the delicious sight of her before very slowly, very deliberately, shucking his jeans and shorts.

Then he reached for the tab on her zipper.

His kisses, Tonya thought as she looked up at the beautiful, naked man leaning over her, were like wine. To a woman used to water, it didn't take many sips to make her drunk. To a woman who'd been deluged with water most of her life, the temptation was too much to deny. She'd known that twelve years ago. She'd known it when he'd given her a taste of his kisses in the lake.

She'd known it when she'd returned to the cabin to see him sitting at the table, even though she'd been telling herself all afternoon that water was all she needed in her life.

Even then, she'd known she was lying. And now, as his strong hands reached for her zipper and slowly slid it down, as his head lowered to press sweet, nipping kisses to the skin he'd revealed, as his tongue circled her navel then followed the line of her zipper, she didn't want to lie any more.

She wanted it all. All the fantasies she'd woven about him through the years, all the sensation his caresses fostered, all the satisfaction her craving for him required. All the wine he offered. It had been so long since she'd felt this way. She was entitled. Just this once to play out a fantasy. Only this time, she had gone into it with her eyes wide open. This was about need. Mutual need and, for tonight, it was enough.

She lifted her hips on a sigh as he gently tugged her jeans down then off her hips. She opened her legs with abandon when he lowered his mouth between them and breathed liquid heat through the wisp of black lace covering her.

With another man, she would have been shy. With another man she would have said no. But she knew this man. She'd known him in countless dreams, in endless fantasies. She trusted him to keep her safe, to take her places she'd never been but desperately wanted to go. And she desperately wanted to go where he was taking her now.

He opened his mouth wide over her, stirring her desire to the flash point, letting her know with a husky growl that he loved the taste of her, the feel of her, the heat of her beneath his mouth. And when he stripped off her panties with a fierce, impatient tug then resettled his broad shoulders between her thighs, she thought she'd implode from the sharp, exquisite pleasure.

One touch of his tongue on her flesh and she felt herself coming, was embarrassed that she was flying so high with such little provocation.

"Web." Breathless, she reached for him, tried to push him away.

He wasn't having any of it. He pushed her hands away, tunneled his palms under her bottom and lifted her toward his busy, busy mouth.

And oh, it was so good. She gave in to it, gave in

to him, to the lavish sensations as he licked and sucked and with unselfish attention to her body's wild responses, drove her up and over the top to an orgasm so perfect and so powerful she couldn't stifle a scream.

Her heart was still slamming out of control, she was still catching her breath when he kissed his way up her body, lingering tenderly at her breasts before lowering his mouth to hers.

He tasted like sex. And like her. And like the heavenly wine he'd just given her as he kissed her deeply and sweetly then pulled away long enough to roll on his protection.

Then he was back. Sleek muscle, satin skin. In one smooth, long thrust, he filled her. In one deep, shocked breath, she took him in. And in the bed that sang along with their love sounds, he pumped steadily into her body and unbelievably took her up again, even higher than the first time.

Whispering his name, whimpering a plea, she clung to him, gasped with him, begged him,. "Please, please, please."

And then she was flying again, soaring with him this time as he thrust one last time, buried his head in her hair and groaned her name as if she was the one thing, the only thing that mattered in his world.

"You're smiling." Web ran a hand down Tonya's bare hip, squeezed gently.

She turned her head on the pillow to look at him. The cabin was bathed in darkness. Only the gentle light from the woodstove they'd started up the last time they'd made it out of bed illuminated his handsome features in the night.

"Is there something you want to share with me?" he prompted when her smile grew.

Tonya couldn't imagine there was anything left that they hadn't shared. They'd made love again after that incredible first time. After they'd roused themselves to eat something then collapsed together back in the soft, squeaky bed and started all over again.

She should be exhausted. She should be embarrassed by some of the things they'd done. She was neither. Instead, she felt more exhilarated than she had at any time in her life. And that's why she was smiling.

He'd raised up on an elbow beside her, his head propped in his hand. The other hand...oh, the other hand, was busy caressing and petting and sending little shivers of the most wonderful sensations up and down her body.

"You're not going to tell me?"

"Why I'm smiling?"

He nodded.

"I was just thinking about inadequacies."

When he frowned she laughed. "A couple of days ago you mentioned something about not being used to feeling inadequate. I was thinking about just how adequate you are."

He pinched her hip and she squealed.

"Okay. More than adequate."

The springs sang as he collapsed to his back, threw

his hands above his head. "A ringing endorsement if I ever heard one."

She turned toward him, cupped his jaw in her palm. "Superbly adequate. Excellently adequate. Exceedingly adequate. Stupendously adequate."

"Yeah, well, I am a guy." He grinned. "And what we just did kind of highlights the old this is why a girl needs a guy thing—one reason why a girl needs a guy anyway. There are many reasons."

Yes, there were. She told herself she'd be satisfied with this one. And then she told him. "I'm content with this one."

He laughed. "I guessed as much when you screamed."

She felt herself flush pink all over.

"Hey," He caught her chin in his hand. "It was beautiful. You were beautiful. You are beautiful."

He tucked her under his shoulder then rested his chin on the top of her head. It was one of those perfect peaces and she simply drifted for a while and enjoyed it. She was almost asleep when he spoke again, all the while threading his fingers through her hair.

"Have you thought about that night? The night of the Christmas party?"

She opened her eyes, swallowed. She hadn't thought about anything but this particular moment since he'd dragged her out of her chair and tossed her on the bed. She didn't want to think about anything else. Not tonight. Tomorrow would be soon enough to face reality. And the reality was, this was a one-time thing. They had no future. He lived in New York

City. She lived wherever her work took her. And that was just for starters.

"I have," he said, interrupting her dismal thoughts. His voice had gone all rusty and soft. Beneath her cheek, his heart beat steady and slow. "I remember so many things about that night. It was bitter cold. Too cold to snow yet frost drifted down from window ledges and sparkled like your eyes. You have such pretty eyes, Tonya."

"I do?" She still thought of herself as the girl behind the glasses even though it had been five years since she'd had laser surgery.

He kissed her temple. "Over the years, I've thought about the way you looked at me that night. I've thought about how soft you were in my arms. About how special you felt. About the taste of you. I've been wanting to taste you again for twelve years."

"You didn't even recognize me when you first arrived," she pointed out.

He chuckled and nuzzled her neck. "Yeah, well. You have to admit, you do look different. A lot different. Plus I was on a mission. I guess you could say I was focused on that."

She went very still as a sudden ugly thought spilled through her head and right out of her mouth. "If this is about the contract—"

"Whoa. Stop right there." He lifted up on an elbow again and looked her directly in the eye. "In the beginning," he admitted, "everything was about the contract. I won't deny it. Feeding the bears, cutting the wood, cooking dinner…it was all about the contract. Do I still want you to sign? Damn right.

"But this," he said, lowering his head and kissing her with slow and thorough intent, "is about you and me and some personal business that's been unfinished for twelve long years."

Dizzied by his kiss, she blinked up at him. "You really thought about me all that time?"

Web smiled, delighted she'd been so easily sidetracked from talk of the contract and charmed by her uncertainty. Her guilelessness was the real thing. She didn't realize how desirable she was.

"I did. I'd told myself that if I ever ran into you again, I'd kiss you just to prove to myself that no kiss could have been as good as the one we shared in the back of the cab that night."

He could see her pulse fluttering at her throat now. "And was it?"

His throat felt thick suddenly and when he managed to speak, it was in a rusty whisper. "It was even better. And you are incredible."

She turned those blue eyes to his and in them he saw all the lingering passion and longing he felt.

"Web—"

He touched two fingers to her lips. They were dewy soft, like the look in her eyes, like the fingertips touching his wrist.

He turned his face into her palm. "We aren't nearly finished with this. You know that, don't you?"

She nodded against his palm, and then sank into sweet sensation when he drew her beneath him again.

Nine

When Web next woke, it was morning. Or at least he assumed it was. It was daylight, in any event. Last night, however, was a pleasant blur of silky skin, surrendering sighs and giving heat.

And now it was the morning after.

He rolled to his back, dragged a hand across his stubbled jaw and hoped he hadn't abraded her tender skin with his beard.

And then he thought of making love with her. The bed still smelled of her. And of sex. He rarely found himself in a woman's bed the morning after. He made it a point not to let it happen. Of course, he'd always made it a point not to get involved with a woman who might have illusions about asking him to hang around for coffee and cozy talk.

The situation being what it was, though, he'd had little choice in the matter. Still, he found himself entertaining a thought that if he *had* had a choice, he might have ended up staying anyway.

Dismissing that fleeting and troubling thought, he sat up, swung his feet to the floor and smelled coffee.

Bless her.

He stretched and rose and, spotting his boxers on the floor, dragged them on. Tonya wasn't anywhere to be seen. And as he poured himself a cup of coffee and swallowed that first eye-opening jolt of caffeine, he wondered what that meant—if anything.

Had she made herself scarce because she was also skittish about mornings after? He leaned a hip against the counter and crossed his ankles, staring broodily at the closed cabin door. If she was skittish, he was relatively certain it was because she had had little experience in the matter, not because she preferred to avoid the situation.

Sweet Tonya of the soft breasts and catchy little sighs, while exuberant and uninhibited and unbelievably responsive, was not all that experienced in the sexual arena. Her reactions had been too pure, too spontaneous and too filled with wonder to have been practiced or polished.

On one hand, he thought, taking his coffee with him into the bathroom where his immediate need was for a shower, he was pleased as hell that he had been the first man to introduce her to some of the pleasures they'd shared last night. On the other, it made him feel like a jaded opportunist.

His original take on her twelve years ago had been dead-on accurate. She was a forever kind of woman. And he was not a forever kind of man.

"And why didn't you think about that last night when you led with your libido?" he muttered aloud, suddenly sobered by the reality.

Hell. What had he done?

With or without the contract, he'd go on his way and she'd go hers, he told himself grimly as he stepped under the hot spray and ducked his head under the water. He hoped it wouldn't hurt her. Hurting her was something he hadn't wanted to do.

Double hell.

Well, there was nothing to be done for it now. He got all twitchy just thinking about being tied to one woman. He wouldn't be good at it. No one in his family was. His grandfather had stayed married to his grandmother for fifty years but he'd kept a stable full of mistresses on the side. His father hadn't been any better at fidelity with any of his four—or was it five?—wives. At least he'd divorced them. Or they'd divorced him, he could never remember. And his mother, well, whether she felt the need to one-up his father or if she was simply fickle, had racked up her share of ex's as well.

It wasn't in the Tyler genes to stay faithful or married to one person. His own personal experience had taught him, he reminded himself as he twisted off the faucets and grabbed a towel, that there had never been a woman he'd seriously considered as a life partner.

He heard the cabin door open and close.

He wiped the steam from the small mirror and glared at his reflection. Where moments ago he'd been content, now he was disgusted. "Had to seduce her, didn't you, Ace? Just had to do it."

On a deep breath, he wrapped the towel around his hips and dragged his shaving gear out of his kit. She'd be wondering if he'd heard her. Wondering what he'd have to say this morning. Wondering how he felt. About her. About them.

And that was the crux of the problem. There could be no them. And he had the guts of a gnat at the moment because, for the life of him, he didn't know what to say to her when he faced her.

Tonya heard the water running in the bathroom and breathed a sigh of relief. Well, at least temporary relief. She just couldn't be blasé about this. She hadn't experienced too many mornings after in her life—and she'd never experienced a night like they'd shared in that bed.

Her cheeks flamed red. The heat quickly spread to her fingers and toes.

She'd gone to bed with Web Tyler. She'd made love with Web Tyler and it had felt like love. Of course, it hadn't been. He was skilled, that was all. He knew how to make a woman respond.

Another spark of red-hot desire fired from her breast to her belly at a particular memory of his amazingly skilled mouth. Oh, did he know how to make a woman respond.

She'd never been a screamer. But then, she'd never

been with him. He'd said it was beautiful. He'd said she was beautiful. Well, in the cool, clear light of day, all she felt was foolish.

Foolish for falling in love with him twelve years ago. Foolish for nursing a crush all this time. Foolish for letting last night happen with no more provocation than a look from his smoldering brown eyes.

The only thing more foolish would be if she let herself fall in love with him again. Thank God that hadn't happened, she thought with a faint sinking in her chest.

On a worried breath, she crossed to the sink to wash her hands. The phone rang at the same time that Web opened the bathroom door.

Startled, because it had been quiet for so many days, she jumped. Or was it because seeing Web dressed made her think about last night?

"Hello. Charlie Erickson's residence."

"Hello little girl."

Charlie's gruff voice, sounding much stronger than the last time she'd heard it rumbled across the line like a distant freight train.

"Charlie!" Delighted to hear him sound so good, she gripped the phone with both hands. "How are you?"

"Bored to death."

"That's a good sign."

"Damn right. I'm fit as a fiddle but they won't let me out of here for another week yet. Something about some cardiac rehab or some other lame excuse to get more money out of my insurance company."

"I'm glad to hear they're taking good care of you," she said, smiling at his sputtering.

"So what's going on out there? Haven't heard from you in a while."

She explained about the storm taking both the electric and phone lines out.

"Figured it was something like that. You find the generator and get it running?"

She stole a glance at Web who was pouring himself a mug of coffee. "Yes. It's working fine. Hopefully I won't need it much longer. They'll surely get the lights on soon now that the phone is working."

They talked about his bears for a while then, his main concern, and, after a promise to come and see him as soon as the roads were cleared, she hung up.

"Good news?" Web asked over the steam rising from his coffee.

"Well, he sounded good. Stronger anyway."

It was much easier to talk about Charlie than last night. "They'll release him next week if he continues to improve."

"You know, at his age, there's every possibility he could have another attack, or that he won't recover sufficiently to live out here on his own."

She did know. And both thoughts had been bothering her. "I guess we'll cross that bridge when we come to it."

"I wonder if he's given any thought—long-term, I mean—to a solution for the bears."

She let out a deep breath. This was also something that concerned her. "I doubt it. And it is a problem.

The bears are dependent on him now for food and will be for as long as they continue to live in these woods. Bears transfer memories from generation to generation. In other words,'' she added at his puzzled look, ''the bears that started eating here forty years ago, pass their memories on to their offspring and they pass it to their offspring and on and on. The cycle will never break.''

''So someone will always have to feed them?''

''Unfortunately, yes.''

''So if Charlie can't return, or if and when he dies—I know it's hard to contemplate,'' he added, and she knew it was in response to her involuntary grimace, ''but he is eighty—the bears will be on their own.''

''Or not,'' she said quietly, finally saying aloud what she'd been thinking.

The shock on his face said he understood. ''You're not serious? You're thinking of taking his place?''

She shrugged. ''Until I can figure out another option.

''I've gotten to know them, too,'' she pointed out when he scowled. ''I can't just leave them to fend for themselves. Or turn them loose on the locals for that matter. They'll look for food elsewhere if they don't find it here which means they'll do property damage because they aren't afraid of approaching humans.''

He dragged a hand through his hair. ''What about the local government? Surely there's a department of natural resources or something that could help out.''

She shook her head. ''Unless they find a wounded

or sick bear, which they'll treat, they'll let nature take its course. In this case, many of the bears will either starve or get shot—either by hunters or by people protecting their property.''

He didn't understand. She could see it in his eyes. He didn't understand how anyone could live this life—live *her* life. And now he was probably wondering what had ever compelled him to make love to her last night.

''About last night,'' she said, digging deep for the backbone to get it out in the open. ''It was very special,'' she said carefully. ''And I loved it. Let's not complicate things with regrets and guilt and second thoughts, okay?''

Web didn't know whether to hug her or shake her or walk out the door. She'd saved him the trouble of a similar speech and let him off the hook. He should be happy as hell. But he wasn't. And she was the last person he'd ever figured to use those particular lines—lines he'd almost perfected to an art form— and blow him off.

And that's exactly what she was doing. He knew because he'd said the same thing, in various forms, every time he left a woman's bed.

Until now.

And now, it was a woman who was saying it to him.

He didn't particularly like hearing it. Not from her.

Talk about the ultimate irony.

So. The big question was why? Why was it bothering him? Why didn't he just give her a hug, thank

her for understanding and thank his lucky stars he
didn't have to talk his way out of a sticky situation?

Because you're in love with her, Ace.

The truth hit him like a 747 breaking the sound
barrier.

He was in love with her. He was in love. For the
first time in his life.

The realization was so huge and so shocking, he
didn't know what to do with it. All he knew was that
he had to get away from her so he could think.

"I'll just go check on the generator," he croaked
and made a beeline for the door.

He had to get out of there. Had to clear his head.
His thick head.

The blood was rushing through his ears so fast and
his breath was backing up so far in his chest that by
the time he got to the shed and threw open the door,
he had to lean against the wall to hold himself upright.

"This is a fine kettle of fish you've gotten me into,
Ollie," he muttered aloud.

He dragged an unsteady hand over his face. He'd
gone and fallen in love with her.

Talk about a kick in the pants.

What was he going to do now?

He hadn't had long to think about it when Tonya
screamed his name.

"Web!"

There was so much anxiety, so much pain in her
shout, he barely recognized the voice as hers. He recognized panic when he heard it, though.

He tore out of the building at a run and found her faced off with the biggest bear he'd ever seen in his life.

"It's Damien," Tonya cried, frozen to the spot.

Web ran to her, then pushed her behind him and out of reach of the bear's dangerous teeth and claws. The animal was stumbling around the compound like a drunk. He ran into a boulder, swatted wildly at a food pan, then rose on his back feet and knocked a bird feeder to the ground with a staggering blow.

Web had snagged a hammer—the first thing he'd seen that looked like a weapon—on his rush to get to her. He held it at the ready, hoping he could get a few licks in if the bear attacked. At least he might be able to afford Tonya a chance to escape.

"No!" she shouted and grabbed his wrist. "Don't hit him. He's hurt. Look."

The blood registered at the same time as she edged out from behind him, tears running down her cheeks.

"He's been shot."

It sure looked that way. The big bear's thick black coat was matted at his shoulder; thick, dark blood oozed from an open wound as he collapsed to all fours, then stumbled a few feet, his head hanging low and swaying from side to side.

"Go to the cabin. Hurry. Get Charlie's gun off the rack on the wall. See if you can find some shells."

"You can't shoot him." The tears were coming fast now as she clutched at his sleeve.

"I don't want to but this could get ugly fast. He's

wounded. He's in pain. He'll strike out at anything and I won't let him hurt you. Now go. Get the gun.

"Go!" he yelled and shoved her toward the cabin when she hesitated. Eyes never leaving the bear, he backed slowly away when the wounded animal emitted a low, weary growl that turned to a roar of anger and pain.

Web had gone as far as the bottom cabin step when the bear heaved a huge, rattling breath and collapsed. Behind him, he heard the cabin door open and close, quickly followed by the rapid intake of Tonya's breath.

Though it was a cool fall day, Web was sweating. He could feel it trickle between his shoulder blades and bead on his forehead as he carefully approached the downed animal.

Blood pumped from the wound at an alarming rate. He was dying. Web was sure of it. If not from blood loss, from shock.

Tonya knew it, too. "We can't just let him die."

Short of a miracle, Web didn't see any option. Then he looked at her face. Tears streaked down her cheeks. Her eyes were filled with a pain so raw and real, it ripped through him like a knife.

And he couldn't bear it. He couldn't bear to see her in this much pain.

"See if Charlie's got any emergency vet numbers. Surely he's had to treat other wounded bears in forty years. Tell them they'll need to chopper in. And tell them we'll make it worth their while. Tell them I'll double their normal fee if they get here within an hour.''

She ran back inside. And as he worked his way a little closer to the downed bear, he heard her speaking rapidly on the phone.

What a man wouldn't do in the name of love, he thought, and understood the wisdom behind the old cliché. Another one also came to mind. There's a fool born every minute.

''And you're one of the biggest, Ace,'' he muttered under his breath as he came within touching distance of an animal that even in this weakened condition could snap his neck with one swing of his powerful foreleg if he chose to.

Its breathing was shallow and fast. Shock from blood loss. Web knew enough basic first aid to see that. He also knew that if he didn't stop the blood flow, Damien would be dead before help arrived.

''Okay big guy,'' he said softly. ''This is between you and me. Me—I'm basically a coward. Big hairy critters are not my bailiwick.''

The bear slogged out a breath, made a noise that sounded almost human. A human sound of pain.

''That's her word, not mine,'' he said and with his heart beating in his throat, kneeled at the bear's back. ''So no critique is necessary. No quick moves, either, okay? And let's hope you've figured out by now that I'm trying to help.''

He shrugged out of his shirt, wadded it up, and with adrenaline pumping like crazy, leaned forward and pressed the shirt to the wound.

The bear heaved, raised his head then let it drop. And Web damn near lost his lunch.

But he stayed where he was, slowly applying a little more pressure, then a little more, until his shirt was soaked with blood.

"They're coming," Tonya said quietly from behind him.

He hadn't even heard her approach.

"Get me some towels," he said quietly and dropped to his knees so he could get better leverage.

Again, he wasn't aware of her leaving or coming back as he continued to apply pressure. When she handed a rolled-up towel over his shoulder, he gingerly lifted his blood-soaked shirt, saw that the blood flow had slowed fractionally and replaced his shirt with his towel.

This time, he put his weight into it and prayed the bear would stay passed out. Within a few minutes, the flow of blood had slowed considerably.

"That's good, right?" Tonya said anxiously from behind him.

"Yeah. Yeah, it's good," he said and then hoped he was right since it could mean one of two things. He'd either succeeded in slowing the blood loss, or the bear had no more blood to lose.

"Did they say how long before they could get here?"

"Thirty minutes. After I tripled their fee. I'll make up the difference," she added quickly.

He couldn't help but grin. He sobered abruptly as

he watched the lifeless bear. He was still breathing but that was the only sign of life.

"Let's just hope they get here in time," he said and pressed on the wound until his arms ached.

"I can take over for you for a while."

He ducked his head to wipe his forehead on his arm. "You stay back. He could come around any time and I don't want you getting hurt. Besides. No point in both of us getting messed up. How about you make a target out of sheets or something for the chopper so they'll know exactly where to set down?"

A mosquito buzzed his ear as he turned his head and watched her race back to the cabin to get the sheets. He let the bastard land. Let it bite. He was afraid to let up on the pressure.

His arms were getting shaky and he was sweating like a butcher when he heard the *whup whup whup* of the chopper blades.

Still, he held steady on the pressure and didn't let go until the vet's assistant relieved him.

"Now we wait," he said, standing back while the professionals did their job.

It was a long shot, the vet had said, but he'd give it his best. He'd arrived via the Department of Natural Resources chopper with a forest ranger piloting. After they'd stabilized Damien, Web had helped them haul the bear into the chopper with the help of a winch and a cattle sling.

"If he makes it, it's because of what you did for him," Tonya said to Web as they watched the helicopter disappear above the tree line. It was headed for Minneapolis where the medical staff at the zoo's hospital was standing by.

He lifted a hand to brush back his damp hair then stopped in midair when he saw it was covered with dried blood. So was his chest and his pants. "If he makes it, it's because he's one tough customer."

"Yeah, well, that's not what the doctor said."

Tonya still couldn't believe what Web had done. He'd risked his own life to save Damien. A wounded bear could be a murderous bear. Web had had no way of knowing whether he'd attack. And she had stood by, panicked to the point of paralysis and had done little to help.

He shrugged and turned toward the cabin. "The DNR guy—Jack, right? He thought they could get a lead on who shot him out of season if they recovered the bullet."

"I hope they nail him to the wall."

"That makes two of us."

"You've started to care about them, haven't you?" she asked quietly. Her chest was full of emotion. Left-over fear for both Damien and Web. Gratitude. Tenderness. And something stronger. Something she still wasn't ready to admit she felt for Web.

He was quiet for a moment. "I've started to care about you," he finally said.

He met her eyes and she could feel her heart rev up in her chest.

"I need a shower."

She stood, her chest tight and watched him go.

I've started to care about you.

Her hand was trembling slightly when she walked to the stove, lit the front burner and set the kettle on to boil. Tea wouldn't settle her nerves, but it would give her something to do other than stare into space and wonder how much stock to put into his words.

Lord help her, she was finally ready to admit she cared about him. Deeply. She loved him. She couldn't deny it any longer. And, at this moment, with him here at the cabin, anything seemed possible.

Was it too much to want? Too much to hope they might have a future?

The phone rang just as the kettle whistled and saved her from pondering the possibilities further.

"Hello, Charlie Erickson's residence."

"Oh, hello." The voice was that of a woman. "I'm so glad someone finally answered. I'm hoping I can reach Web Tyler there."

"Web's here, but he's in the shower at the moment. Would you like to hold on for him or do you have a number where he can call you back?"

"Oh, he knows how to reach me, but I'm not about to ring off after trying for days to make a connection. I'll just hang on. You wouldn't be Ms. Griffin, by any chance?"

"I am, yes."

"Well, hello, dear. So nice to finally talk to you. I'm Pearl. Pearl Reasoner, Web's secretary."

And godmother, Tonya added, smiling at the warmth in Pearl's voice. "Web's mentioned you."

She laughed. "Oh, I'll bet he has. How is our boy?

Grumping and grousing or has he taken my advice and relaxed a bit?''

''A little of both, I'd say,'' Tonya offered honestly and listened as the shower shut off, her heart still a little rattled by his comment and by the look in his eyes when he'd said it.

She turned when the bathroom door opened and Web stepped out, a damp towel knotted at his hips. His hair was wet, his chest still glistened with water droplets and, in his eyes, she saw something she'd always dreamed of seeing when he looked at her.

''For you,'' she said, handing him the phone. ''Your secretary.''

She went back to her brewing tea. She didn't want to intrude but she couldn't help but hear his side of the conversation. She smiled at the honest affection in his voice when he asked after Pearl's health. He grew thoughtful and sober when he responded to questions about various projects that he'd evidently left hanging fire while he was out here trying to sign her to a contract.

The longer he talked, the more it became obvious she'd been deluding herself. He was the CEO of a major publishing corporation. He was a mover and a shaker. Cosmopolitan to the bone. He had nothing in common with a wildlife photographer who hated the burn of concrete beneath her feet and needed wide-open spaces to maintain her equilibrium.

And they had no chance of a future together.

A deadweight settled on her shoulders as reality dawned with a vengeance. She'd known from the onset that they were from different worlds with different wants and needs. Just as she knew that in the real world, love did not conquer all.

She slipped outside while he was deep in a dialogue about editorial staff changes and timetables, and battled back threatening tears.

Ten

―――

Web found Tonya in the shed, filling food pans.

"So, you spoke with Pearl."

"She seemed very sweet." Forcing a smile, she ripped open a sack of feed and dug into it with a scoop.

She was quiet, Web thought. Too quiet.

"Something's wrong."

She shook her head. "Just preoccupied."

"With Damien?"

A tear trailed down her cheek before she could turn away and hide it from him.

He went to her, cupped her shoulders in his hands and turned her to face him. "Hey. It's okay. He's made of tough stuff. He'll pull through."

She drew in a fractured breath, nestled against his chest. "Yeah."

He held her that way for a while, his strong, yet vulnerable warrior woman who got all mushy over a wounded bear. She cared fiercely about those she chose to love. And he knew she loved him. He'd known it almost from the beginning. Which worked out mighty fine since he loved her, too.

He wanted to say it. He wanted to hear it. Now seemed as good a time as any.

"I love you, Tonya."

She went stock still.

He waited in a silence punctuated only by her stilted breath and the distant hum of something that sounded like thunder—which seemed unlikely since the sky was pristine blue.

Finally she pushed out of his arms, brushed the hair back from her face and looked at the floor of the shed.

"Okay, you obviously don't know the drill. I say I love you then—" he paused, made a leading motion with his hand.

Very slowly she shook her head. "This is pointless."

"Pointless?" A slow, slippery nausea fueled by anxiety, rolled through his gut. "I tell you I love you and you tell me it's pointless?"

"You want me to tell you I love you?" Anger colored her words and her cheeks. "Fine. I love you, okay? I love you. But to what end?"

He blinked, pushed out a confused laugh. "Well, the end I had in mind goes something like, and they lived happily ever after."

"And where would this happy life be? New York?"

He frowned and suddenly understood where she was going. Just as he understood her point before she voiced it.

"Your life doesn't mesh with mine, Web," she said, her voice softer now, filled with defeat. "We're both too smart to delude ourselves into thinking we could find a happy medium. Your comfort zone is the city. Mine is here—or places where I can get as far away from congestion as possible."

Her blue eyes pleaded now, as behind them the unmistakable sound of machinery grew louder. "Don't you see? By nature, we're incompatible. By choice we live in separate worlds. And while I'd love to think we could find some way to meet in the middle, I'd be a fool to believe it could really happen. So would you."

It was hard to argue with the truth. She was right. He knew she was right. And still, he couldn't give it up.

"Do you have so little faith in us?"

She looked weary and sad and resigned. "What I have is little faith in love. It's not always enough. And let's be painfully honest here, even if it was, we've had four days together. Two of them fighting. What we feel, what we *think* we feel now, is going to look a lot different when we get past the chemistry."

She touched a hand to his cheek. "I'm sorry."

Then she shoved open the door to the shed and walked outside.

He didn't even know what to say. She was right. About everything. Everything except one very important point. How he felt about her was not going to change. He loved her.

Too much to make her unhappy.

He felt beaten and bruised when he followed her outside. That's when he saw the bulldozer and the bucket truck that indicated the road had been cleared.

If he was a believer in fate, he'd say this was an omen telling him everything she'd said was dead-on right.

"You have pressing issues waiting for you back in New York," she said with so little emotion in her voice it frightened him. "I'll tell the boys you need a ride back to town."

"Quit fussing over me, little girl. I'm old but I'm not dead."

Charlie was right. She was fussing. Tonya knew it but couldn't seem to help herself. He'd been home four days now and even though he grew stronger every day, the heart attack had taken its toll. He'd lost weight. His color still bore that hospital pallor. And he still tired quickly.

"If I didn't fuss, you wouldn't have anyone to grouse and complain to. How much fun would that be for you?"

Charlie made a hrumphing sound. "Makes a man

wonder how he lived so many years alone what with all you females bandying about like mother hens.''

He was saving face by grumbling about Helga. Tonya knew that he secretly enjoyed the elderly woman's attention when she came to visit armed with healthy casseroles, vegetables and fresh fruits.

All in all, things were going well. Charlie was back home. Word from the Minneapolis zoo was that Damien had turned a corner and was expected to recover. Blood loss and shock had been the major problems as the bullet hadn't hit any vital organs. With time and luck, they should be able to rehabilitate him and return him to Charlie's refuge. The DNR also had a lead on who had tried to hunt out of season.

She'd sent her last batch of photos to her agent, who was now in the process of accepting bids from several wildlife magazines.

Yep. Life was great. Life was fine.

And she was miserable.

Web had been gone two weeks. And she'd wanted to chase after him every day since and tell him she was sorry she'd been so frightened of her feelings. That it had been her insecurity talking. That somehow, they would find a way to meet in the middle. After Charlie had come home and told her what Web had done, she knew there had to be a way.

"Didn't know him from Adam when he came to the hospital," Charlie had said while she'd sat there dumbstruck by the story. "He explained who he was, that he'd been at the cabin with you and then he made me an offer I couldn't refuse."

Web had offered Charlie three times what the property was worth, a life lease to live there and a plan to set up a wildlife sanctuary for the bears.

No kidding, Tonya had thought.

"That face gets much longer someone's gonna slap asphalt on it and make it into a road," Charlie said, snapping her back to the moment. "Go get him, girl."

She stared at the kindly old bear of a man and realized she hadn't given him nearly enough credit for being intuitive. She hadn't said a word about Web and their relationship. Obviously, she hadn't hidden her feelings well, either.

"Go get him," he repeated. "I'll call Helga to come over. She and I can take care of the chores. And by the time I get tired of listening to her lectures on healthy food and moderate exercise and give her the boot, I'll be back to my old self again. Go on," he insisted. "Go fix things."

He was right. She did need to fix things. She only hoped it wasn't too late.

She hugged him. "You're not about to boot her anywhere. You know when you've got a good thing going. Besides you like her."

Another snort.

She smiled. "I'll be back," she promised then ran to throw a few essentials in her backpack.

Web had been smelling mosquito spray in his sleep. When he slept, that was, which wasn't often.

It had been a week since he'd left Minnesota. A week in which he'd tried to convince himself he was as happy as hell to be out of there. As content as a damn clam that the beat of the city regulated his life again, not the sway of the wind or the rise of the moon. Or the siren call of a blue-eyed blonde who he couldn't get out of his head to save his soul.

If he could just quit thinking about her. About the desire in her eyes when he'd filled her. About the feel of her skin beneath his lips.

About the scent of her mosquito spray, he thought again sourly as the scent wafted toward his nostrils again. The thought was ridiculous, since he was sitting behind his desk on the twenty-eighth floor of his Sixth Avenue office.

He heard his door open.

"Not now, Pearl," he said without looking up.

"It's not Pearl. And if it's not a good time, I'll wait until it is."

His head jerked up. And there she was. The woman of his dreams in her camouflage shorts, her skinned-up knees and smelling wonderfully, beautifully, faintly of mosquito spray. He'd never seen anything so beautiful in his life.

There he was, Tonya thought, the man of her dreams sitting behind his desk, looking sophisticated, distant, a little haggard and a lot haunted in his designer suit and tie. She'd never seen anything so beautiful in her life.

"If…if this is a bad time—"

"No. No. It's fine." He was watching her as if he didn't know whether to stand or run or stay exactly where he was. In the end, that's what he did. He sat there. Lord of his universe. Master of his domain. She thought of Damien in the wild. They were both strong males from two different worlds, and yet fate had drawn them together. Surely she should be able to figure out a way to bridge the gap, as well.

"You bought Charlie's property," she began without preamble. "You went to the hospital before you flew back to New York, cut a deal with him to purchase it for three times what it's worth, then you made provisions for him to stay on as long as he likes. You put the wheels in motion to have the property legally declared a wildlife refuge and set up an account to insure there will always be staff to man it."

He blinked. "And?"

"Why? Why would you do that?"

"I figure there will be a buck or two in it for me someday."

She walked over to his desk praying that the look she saw in his eyes was still love. Needing it to be love more than she'd ever needed anything in her life. "I think you did it because you're a nice guy."

"That's a nasty rumor. I have no idea how it got started."

"I think you did it because you found the bears as irresistible as I did. I think you did it because you love me."

The pulse at his throat leaped and his breath stalled before he manufactured a scowl. "I believe I might have mentioned that. You still gave me the boot."

Her heart swelled and grew. "Yeah, well. I never said I was the sharpest tack in the drawer."

He leaned back in his luxurious leather chair and steepled his hands in front of his mouth. "Is that what you came here to say?"

So, he was going to play hardball. She was up for it. "I came to apologize."

"For?"

"For making decisions about us based on my insecurities."

He lifted a shoulder and while he appeared the picture of indifference, something in his eyes told her he wasn't nearly as unmoved by her presence as he wanted her to think.

That's when she realized just how badly she'd hurt him.

"I'm so sorry. I'm so sorry I sold us short. I was a fool to let my biggest fear—opening myself up to a man who might not be able to accept me the way I am—stand in the way of seeing him for the man he really is, a man who is steady and true. A man I can trust with my heart. "

He let out a sigh that sounded suspiciously like relief. "I was stupid to leave and not work harder to convince you."

"So that makes us two foolish, insecure people when it comes to love. I love you, Web."

He closed his eyes tight, then smiled up at her. "Why don't you come over here and say that?"

She didn't hesitate. She walked around his desk when he pushed his chair back and sat down on his lap. Linking her arms around his neck, she smiled into his mocha-brown eyes.

"We can make it work. I see that now. But it's going to take both of us."

"There was never any question in my mind that we could make things work between us." He became quiet then. "You need to know that I'm as scared about this as you are. I might not be any good at this forever-and-always thing. I've never thought I had what it takes to give a woman a future."

"I'm not just any woman."

He chuckled and pressed his forehead to hers. "You've got that right, cupcake."

"And you're not the completely driven power broker you were when you arrived in Minnesota."

"Got that right, too. I was counting on the challenge of a successful launch of a new project to revitalize me, and here all I needed was you. Someone who would make me be the best man I could possibly be."

"You are the best man you could possibly be."

He held her hard against him. Buried his hands in her hair, all traces of teasing gone. "God, I missed you."

She felt a tear threaten, but, as he so often did, he shifted gears and made her smile again.

"We can discuss my stellar character later. Right now, I need to get my hands on you. On all of you," he clarified, lifting her off his lap. He took her hand and dragged her toward his office door.

"Cancel my afternoon appointments," he said to a

grinning Pearl as they breezed by her desk at a fast trot.

"How about I just cancel tomorrow's, too, while I'm at it?" Pearl suggested with a wink at Tonya.

"That's why she's my executive secretary," Web said, grinning as he punched the elevator button. "She knows what I need before I do."

"I know what you need, too," Tonya whispered when the elevator doors closed and he pulled her into his arms for a long, hungry kiss.

Tonya laughed when Web lowered the privacy screen in his limo then dragged her into his arms. Then they necked like teenagers all the way to his SoHo co-op.

"There's only one thing keeping me from making love to you right here, right now," he murmured as he dragged his mouth along her jaw and pressed her back against the luxurious leather upholstery. "The ride is too short and I want to take my sweet time with you."

"That works out real well." She knotted his hair in her hands and pulled his mouth down to hers. "Because I've got nothing but time."

When they reached his co-op and Web led her inside, Tonya was aware of flashes of color, the glint of chrome, tall, slim windows and the feel of his hand tugging her shirttails out of her shorts.

"I thought you said something about taking your time," she said with a laugh as he struggled with the buttons on her shirt.

"I believe that's called nit-picking. And we've got all afternoon. And all night to take it slow."

"And all day tomorrow."

"And a lot of time to make up for." His eyes turned dark and hot. Starting now.

"Pink. Thank God," he said, when he finally undid the last button and discovered her lacy bra underneath the shirt. "Do you know how many times I've thought about pink lace and you and nothing else?"

"How many?" she asked, unzipping her shorts, slipping them down her hips and revealing panties that matched her bra.

"Too many." His breath caught. He reached for her. "Come here."

He bit her bare shoulder gently. And walked her backward toward the bedroom.

"You've been working hard, I see," he said between kisses when he spotted a fresh scrape on her knee. He pressed a kiss there. Another to the bruise on her arm. "Any other spots I should kiss and make better?"

"Here," she whispered, touching a spot just under her jaw. "I really need a kiss here."

He was more than happy to comply.

"How about here?" he murmured, pressing her to her back on the bed and following her down. He tracked a string of kisses down her throat, gently nipped the ridge of her collarbone, then nuzzled under the lacy edge of her bra.

"Umm. Yes. There more than ever. I've done some dreaming, too."

His gaze on her face, he unhooked her bra, then bent over her, taking her nipple into his mouth.

It was all sensation then. So much it stole her breath. So intense it ravaged her senses. His mouth was everywhere. His hands skated across her bare skin. A soft caress. An urgent plea.

"I love you," he whispered, moving back to her breast and drawing her deep into his mouth. So deep she felt a pull low in her belly that intensified the ache, fired the burn.

"I...need...Web...please. I need you down here with me. And I need you to get out of those clothes."

He laughed at the frustration in her voice. And she loved the sound, loved the look on his face as he knelt above her and shrugged out of his shirt.

"That," he said, reaching for his belt, "can be arranged."

"You better believe it can."

She helped him with the zipper on his slacks, then waited for what seemed like forever until he finished undressing and joined her on the bed.

Heat against heat, skin against skin.

She traced the corded muscles of his back with her fingers. Explored the shadow of a day's growth of beard on his jaw. Absorbing his textures, memorizing his scent.

"You feel so good," she whispered against his throat.

"And you feel incredible."

She cupped his head in her hands and pulled him

toward her for a kiss that was all soft lips, wet heat and delirious sensation.

And then he was on his back, lifting her above him. Finding her heat with his fingers, he stroked her, praising her wetness, driving her wild with wanting him.

As he reached for protection in the drawer, she took him in her hands. "I want your babies."

The emotion in his eyes brought tears to hers as he lowered her onto his straining erection then let her take him home.

He reached for her breasts, squeezed reverently as she rode him to a slow and sultry rhythm that matched the cadence of the words she couldn't keep inside any longer. "I love you. I have always loved you. I will always love you."

"I can't get over how beautiful it is up here."

Web loved the delight in Tonya's eyes as her gaze drank in his rooftop garden.

"My contribution to the ecosystem."

"So, you've got a little nature boy in you, after all."

"I guess there's a little of something in all of us," he agreed, walking over to her and pulling her into his arms. He couldn't resist. She looked insanely adorable in his white dress shirt. Which was all she was wearing next to the skin he'd stroked and petted and kissed only minutes ago, and couldn't wait to get his hands on again.

She laid her head against his chest. Sighed with contentment.

"You know," he said, dropping a kiss to the crown of her head, "there are over five hundred varieties of wildlife inhabiting Central Park."

"I'd heard that," she said coyly. "Sounds like a dream job for a wildlife photographer."

He sobered abruptly, set her away from him and with his hands on her upper arms, met her gaze. "We can make this work, Tonya. I won't be able to go with you on all the assignments you take, but when I can, I will."

She smiled into his eyes. "Well, since you'll be doling out those assignments, you'll have a heads-up on where I'll be. That is, if your contract offer is still open."

Love. It shined in her eyes, an extension of her heart.

"Don't do that for me."

"I'm doing it for us. And because I don't feel the need to be freelance anymore. I'm strictly a team player now."

He drew her into a bear hug so fierce she laughed and told him he'd break her bones if he didn't ease up.

"I love you," he said, kissing her soundly. "And just so you know, you had another twenty-four hours before I came after you."

"Nice how that worked out, huh?"

"How would you feel about building a little getaway cabin down by the lake for when we go to visit Charlie and the bears?''

Her eyes went all misty and soft. ''I love everything about the idea. Just like I love everything about you.''

''How about we trip on back to the bedroom and you can show me just how much?''

She showed him. Several times by morning.

''You are insatiable,'' he said on an exhausted laugh. Spread-eagled on his back in the middle of the bed, he grinned up at her. ''Where have you been all my life?''

''Waiting,'' she said with so much love in her eyes, he felt it seep into his bones.

He brushed the hair back from her eyes. ''I'm afraid you're going to have to wait again, at least another half hour or so. Unless…''

''Unless?'' she asked, her eyes dancing in response to the mischief in his voice.

''Unless you brought some mosquito spray with you.''

She blinked, shook her head in confusion. ''Well that's a new one.''

''Tell me about it. Every time I get a whiff of it, I think of you and it turns me on.''

She laughed. ''You're really warped, you know that?''

''Yeah. I'm crazy all right. Crazy in love with you. How about we go really crazy and get married?''

She hiked herself up on an elbow. ''Married? You mean it?''

"I've never meant anything more."

"And you're not going to come to your senses and withdraw the offer?"

"Not in a million years."

She smiled. Instant sunshine. "Then yes. Yes! Yes! Yes!" she cried, and launched herself into his arms.

Maybe, he thought as he kissed her, they were just crazy enough that together they could make it work.

* * * * *

THE BODYGUARDS

*They will not only guard your body,
they will steal your heart and fulfill
your deepest desires.
Coming soon from Cindy Gerard
and St. Martin's Press*

Silhouette® Desire®

presents

KING OF HEARTS

You're on his hit list.

Enjoy the next title in

Katherine Garbera's

King of Hearts miniseries:

MISTRESS MINDED
(Silhouette Desire #1587)

When a workaholic boss persuades his faithful
assistant to pretend to be his temporary
mistress, it's going to take the influence of
a matchmaking angel-in-training to bring
them together permanently!

*Available June 2004
at your favorite retail outlet.*

New York Times **Bestselling Author**

LISA JACKSON

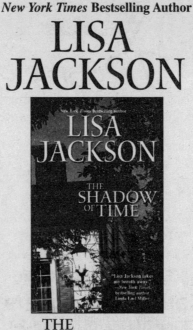

THE
SHADOW
OF TIME

After four long years, Mara Wilcox had finally accepted that her lover, Shane Kennedy, had been tragically killed overseas. But now, inexplicably, he was back—as handsome, arrogant and sensual as ever! Can Mara and Shane overcome the shadow of time and give in to their long-denied passion?

"Lisa Jackson takes my breath away."
—*New York Times* **bestselling author Linda Lael Miller**

Coming in June 2004.

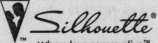

Where love comes alive™

Visit Silhouette at www.eHarlequin.com

PSLJ824

If you enjoyed what you just read,
then we've got an offer you can't resist!

Take 2 bestselling love stories FREE!

Plus get a FREE surprise gift!

COMING NEXT MONTH